Dangerous

Enjoy!
Dick

Previously published:

Novels:

Hustle (1989)
Dangerous Dancing (2000) *
Dangerous Relationships (2001) *
Dangerous Encounters (2003) *
Searching for Rachel (2007) *

Collections (essays, poems, short-stories)

Somewhere Along the Way (2004)
Tomorrow is Just Another Road (2011)
Derring-do (2016)
Vanished (Stories of the Unexpected) (2004)

Numerous magazine articles appearing in:

Del Webb monthly magazine
Cane Bay Living magazine

- Featuring Nick Alexander

Dangerous

7 Short Mysteries

Richard Standring

Copyright © 2023 by Richard Standring.
Cover art by Secoura/Pixabay
Interior artwork by Dave Williams

Library of Congress Control Number: 2023909369
ISBN: Hardcover   978-1-6698-7761-5
            Softcover   978-1-6698-7763-9
            eBook   978-1-6698-7762-2

All rights reserved. No part of this book may be reproduced or transmitted in any form or by any means, electronic or mechanical, including photocopying, recording, or by any information storage and retrieval system, without permission in writing from the copyright owner.

This is a work of fiction. Names, characters, places and incidents either are the product of the author's imagination or are used fictitiously, and any resemblance to any actual persons, living or dead, events, or locales is entirely coincidental.

Any people depicted in stock imagery provided by Getty Images are models, and such images are being used for illustrative purposes only.
Certain stock imagery © Getty Images.

Print information available on the last page.

Rev. date: 05/18/2023

To order additional copies of this book, contact:
Xlibris
844-714-8691
www.Xlibris.com
Orders@Xlibris.com
853235

For Marcia

Contents

Introduction ix

Dangerous Dancing 1
Dangerous Relationships 20
Dangerous Consequences 46
Dangerous Intentions 62
Dangerous Encounters 70
Dangerous Flirtations 85
Dangerous Waters 93

About The Author, Richard Standring 133

Introduction

*D*eception wears a mask to hide the identity of a person who may not be what you see. That is the underlying theme for several stories.

There are five short-stories and two flash fiction pieces. Those two were re-edited from prior short stories. The idea being that a short story can be reduced by editing and still maintain the element of suspense.

It was a challenge. What I learned, shorter can oftentimes be better.

If these stories were labeled murder mysteries, it would be giving away too much. A word of caution, this is **adult fiction**. I've kept the vulgarity to a minimum. In the real world, it still exists for which I apologize.

Enjoy.

Richard Standring

Dangerous Dancing

In police jargon, a dancer is a suspect who tries to evade questioning.

Once a month, Detective Sergeant Nick Alexander had the weekend assignment as Duty Officer. Normally, his routine involved robberies, break-ins and sometimes fraud. His Sunday morning routine changed when it was reported that someone drowned at the local marina, apparently falling overboard after some heavy drinking. Neighboring yacht owners reported a party that lasted into late evening, with lots of loud music.

"Looks like an accidental drowning," the responding officer reported.

"How do you think it happened?" Nick asked. He was admiring the 38-foot yacht moored in a slip at the marina where a drowning was a most unusual event. Nick noted the name of the yacht, *Success*.

"Looks like the guy leaned over the back railing, pitched his cookies and fell overboard. There's some of his dried puke on the side."

"Anybody hear or see anything?"

"We're checking now. Must have happened last night. Body has been in the water for a while. Security guy found him while making his routine rounds. Too much to drink is my guess."

"We'll wait on a toxicology report to see just how much booze he consumed." Nick noticed a guest register with six current names. He used his cellphone to photograph the page. "I'd like to have fingerprints taken. Did you touch anything?"

"Why? This is an accidental drowning, not a homicide, Nick."

"Well humor me. When the marina office opens find out who owns this boat. I'd also like to know why this wasn't reported earlier."

The victim's soaking wet body revealed an overweight male who appeared to be in his early-to-mid 50s. When they removed his wallet, they learned his name was Vincent Morada. He was 53. Nick noted the address in Bloomfield Hills, an upscale neighborhood north of Detroit.

He hated having to inform the family, just his luck to have this happen on his watch.

By mid-morning Nick learned the victim was the owner

of the yacht. The marina manager indicated the boat seemed to be used only on weekends for entertainment. Sometimes it didn't leave the slip. DMV records indicated that Vincent owned a Lincoln Continental President edition. They found it parked in the private marina parking lot. Nick found a briefcase and business cards. He learned Vince was a sales representative for a prominent business publication. *That might explain the need to entertain clients.*

Vince's wife, Emily answered the door. Unlike her husband, she had a small frame, a pleasant smile and natural gray hair.

"Why would the police show up here on a Sunday?" she asked after seeing Nick's badge.

"May I come in?" Nick asked.

"Of course. Is this about Vince? Was he in an accident?"

"Can we sit down?"

"Oh dear, this must be some bad news."

"I'm very sorry to inform you that your husband drowned last night at the marina."

"How did it happen?"

"It appears he was drinking, possibly too much. It looks like he was leaning over the railing to puke and must have lost his balance. He fell into the water. His head must have hit one of the support pilings, I noticed an abrasion on his forehead. We'll know more when the coroner issues his report."

Emily and Nick were sitting in the living room when a very attractive woman with red hair entered the room. Emily remained stoic, dabbing tears.

"This is Ruth Lambert, Vince's assistant. Vince has his office here."

"Is something wrong?" Ruth asked looking from Emily to Nick.

"Yes, apparently Vince had an accident yesterday, or last night on the boat. He's dead!"

"Oh, how awful! What happened? I was on the boat yesterday afternoon. We were entertaining a few clients," Ruth said.

"Perhaps you can help clear up a few things since you were there. I saw the guest register; your name didn't appear on it."

"No, that's because I wasn't a guest. More like a hostess, helping Vince."

"What time did you leave?"

"It was around eight-thirty."

"Were any of the guests still there?"

"We were all leaving about the same time. Vince had a lot to drink. He left the party to lay down. He was sleeping when I left."

Nick opened a small notebook and jotted the time Ruth said she left. He had a lot more questions and was glad she was there. *He also wondered why would she be at the office on Sunday?*

"Your husband must be very successful to own a big yacht like that."

"Yes he is, sorry; was successful. My family comes from money and two years ago, I bought that boat for Vince for his birthday. He's been wanting a boat for some time to entertain his clients. Now, I wish I hadn't bought it!"

A door opened and a young woman rushed in, running over to Emily. "Mom, is everything alright?"

"Your father died last night on the boat. This police officer just gave us the news."

"Was Ruth with him when he died?"

"No," Ruth interjected. "He was sleeping soundly when I left. He'd been heavily drinking all afternoon. We're just now getting the report."

"So, was it a heart attack?" the daughter asked Nick.

Nick stood up. He was facing Emily and her daughter. Emily was repeating what Nick reported. "I'll be in touch as soon as we know more." He felt Ruth touch his shoulder and he turned.

"I'll walk you out," she whispered.

They were standing beside Nick's police vehicle. Nick asked, "I didn't catch the daughter's name."

"It's Lynn. Lynn Marie. Emily should have introduced you. She's upset and trying hard not to show it. And, before you ask, I'll explain she hates me if you didn't pick up on that. She thinks her father is infatuated with me and that we're having an affair."

"I can see where that would upset her. Are you? Having, or were you having an affair with Vince?" *Nick could believe it.*

"Of course not! Emily and I have become good friends. She likes to visit me in the office. Brings me tea and we chat when Vince is out."

"Tell you what, let me get my briefcase and purse and let's meet at Dunkin' Doughnuts on Michigan for some coffee because this may take a while to explain."

Nick liked that suggestion. In fact, it was as if she was reading his mind. He could see why the daughter might suspect her father of being infatuated. Ruth looked like a model, had a lot of poise and had that take-charge attitude. Some of Nick's questions would border on the personal side. *Vince's unfortunate accident opened the door for Nick to meet someone new, someone exciting, someone he wanted to know better.*

In the doughnut shop, Ruth sat at a table opposite Nick. She boldly placed a hand over Nick's in a manner that caused him to relax and at the same time, made him wonder about her personal life. He didn't see a ring to indicate she was married or engaged. Despite the interruption of his normal Sunday routine, Nick felt no reason to hurry through this discussion. His male hormones began to respond when Ruth's hand covered his. It was subtle…and sexy!

"What brought you to the office today?" Nick asked.

"I left my briefcase in the office and stopped by to pick it up. I confess I was a little worried when I saw your car in the driveway."

"Is it awkward for you to work in an office at home?"

"It was at first. However, Emily made me feel part of the family. She's a very sweet lady as you must have noticed. Too bad her daughter isn't more like her."

"How long have you worked for Vince?"

"Going on two years. He was looking for an assistant and I applied for the job. He hired me immediately. Vince plays a lot of golf with clients at the country club. I'm responsible for keeping his appointment schedule. Sometimes he has to make a presentation. Now that I've learned a few things he relies on me to help him. What about you, Nick? Do you like your job?"

"It keeps me busy. I don't do patrol work. Mostly, I'm involved with criminal activity."

"Then why would you have an interest in an accidental drowning?"

"As luck would have it, this is my weekend as duty officer. Otherwise, I would not be involved." *And I would not have had an opportunity to meet you,* he thought.

"So do you investigate murders and stuff like that?"

"Yes, but homicides are few and far between. Break-ins and robberies are more common."

"Are you working on anything special now?"

"Auto thefts seem to be on the rise. It amazes me how many people go shopping and leave their vehicle unlocked."

"That wouldn't matter to a professional car thief, would it? I read somewhere that they can get into a locked car in just a few seconds."

"That's true, but why make it easy for them?"

"Do you prefer Nick or Nicholas?"

"Nick works fine for me."

"Okay, are you married, Nick? I don't see a ring."

"I've been divorced for three years. How about you?"

"Like you, divorced, no kids to cope with. Just a working gal trying to make her way in the world today."

"Sounds like the lyrics to a song. Tomorrow is my day off; would you be interested in having dinner? I know a few good restaurants."

"Yes! I'd be delighted. Funny, I was about to ask you out."

Nick walked Ruth to her car, a bright red Ford Mustang convertible with a tan top. He watched her leave and felt invigorated. Ruth was several notches above some of the waitresses he'd dated.

Back in the office, Nick was thinking about how Vince's unfortunate accident turned out to be a fortunate opportunity for Nick, meeting an extremely sexy woman who would dominate his thoughts for the rest of the day, and tomorrow.

#

Vince's daughter, Lynn picked up the Lincoln at the marina on Monday. There was no reason to impound the vehicle. Before leaving, she entered the boat and gathered some of her father's personal items. She was also checking the beds for evidence of a recent romp. Finding nothing, she still wasn't convinced there was something going on with Ruth and her father. Emily didn't agree with her. The detective gave Ruth the once over while at the house and Lynn had to agree Ruth was a looker. When she asked about the guest register, she was told that Detective Nick Alexander took it. She saw evidence that fingerprints had been taken and wondered why that was necessary.

Now that Vince was gone, the boat was no longer needed. Lynn planned to help her mother find a suitable broker to sell the boat. That thought caused her to look for the boat's documents and logbook. Vince always kept them in a drawer in the cockpit. When she looked, they were missing!

#

Ruth leased a small, one bedroom condo in Birmingham, a 10-minute drive to work. She was waiting for Nick outside when he arrived promptly at six. Nick made reservations at The Fox and Hounds, a popular five-star restaurant in Bloomfield Hills. She met him as soon as he arrived, opening Nick's passenger door. Nick was disappointed she hadn't invited him in. He was interested in seeing her place.

"Sorry about formalities, I'm starved," she said. "Did you know this was one of Vince's favorite haunts?"

"No, I don't know much about him, but I intend to learn more."

"Well, I'll be glad to help you with anything you need. I know most of his clients."

"The six on the guest register is a good starting point. Were they all clients?"

"Three are prospects, the other three are clients. Vince liked to let his better client-type friends brag about their success with the prospects. Sometimes it turned out to be beneficial. What I find interesting is your interest in his clients. Do you always investigate accidents like this?"

"Ruth, everyone is thinking it was an accident. And that might be the case. I won't commit to it until I've explored the situation thoroughly and eliminated other possibilities?"

"Are you thinking something sinister happened?"

"Please don't discuss any of this with Emily. I don't want to upset her. As of this moment, we don't know what happened. It's speculation. It looks like an accident; I just have to satisfy my curiosity. National crime statistics show that in smaller communities like ours, homicides are frequently written off as accidents because the local police often don't have qualified investigators. Sometimes the first responders corrupt the scene unknowingly. Also, the local chamber of commerce wants to keep the crime statistics as low as possible to keep their residents and future residents happy." It was a speech Nick had made numerous times. "I'll know more in a few days after talking with those clients and getting back the fingerprint results."

"You took fingerprints? Ruth looked surprised. "Why?"

"It's routine procedure. I ordered them taken. The results will be back soon. We should probably fingerprint you to eliminate yours from the others we found."

"I'll have to think about that. I've never been fingerprinted." Suddenly the romantic mood shifted. Ruth finished her drink, picked up her wine glass and got up. "Excuse me, I need to use the lady's room." She placed the empty glass on the corner of the bar as she passed by.

It was the last time Nick saw her. Ruth never returned to the table. He waited a half-hour. His detective instincts kicked in and while he was still waiting, he went to the bar got the empty glass before the bartender grabbed it. Nick wrapped the glass in a napkin and asked a hostess to check the ladies' room for Ruth.

"I think she left in an Uber. I saw her leave by the back

entrance to the parking lot at least twenty-minutes ago," she said.

Nick called Ruth's number and left a message. He drove to her condo, knocked on the door. No answer. No red Mustang. All the blinds were closed. He hadn't noticed that when he picked her up for dinner.

On a hunch, Nick called Emily. "By any chance have you heard from Ruth?"

"She was just here and left a few minutes ago with some of her things. She seemed very upset about something. Is there anything I should know?"

"I'm not sure what is happening. I think I may have spooked her. If she shows up for work tomorrow, have her call me."

"I got the impression she isn't coming back. She took her things."

#

The coroner's report arrived on Monday. Vince died from drowning however he suffered a concussion when his head hit a vertical piling supporting the dock where he fell overboard. Time of death was estimated to be around 9:30 PM. And nobody saw or heard anything.

The fingerprint report matched the guest list as well as Vince. Nothing showed for Ruth Lambert. Another set of prints were for a Rita Lawson. A quick follow-up search revealed an open warrant for Rita Lawson in St. Louis, MO for embezzlement and fraud. Nick called the St. Louis police for additional information on Rita Lawson.

"Still an open case. Apparently, she was a personal assistant to some rich guy who was a heavy investor in the stock market. One day he checks on his accounts and finds his entire portfolio has been cashed out and she's disappeared." The description Nick was given matched Ruth Lambert. This situation happened a little over two years ago, about the time Ruth started to work with Vince.

This was more than a coincidence. Nick ordered a police guard for the yacht, Success. The boat was now a possible crime scene. Nick drove to Bloomfield Hills to visit Emily and warn her that some funds might be missing. She should check all Vince's accounts.

He was too late. When he arrived, Emily was crying and shaking.

"I can't believe Ruth would do such a thing. I just called the bank to put a hold on Vince's business account and was told the money was transferred to an international account that is on their watch list. The manager was planning to call Vince about it. He didn't know about Vince's death and asked if the police were involved."

Nick searched Ruth's desk and found nothing of interest. He called his office for someone to come and fingerprint her work area. He was writing notes to himself when he dropped his pen. Getting down on his knees to search for his pen he discovered a picture frame on the floor behind the desk. It was an earlier photo of Ruth standing on a boat between two young men who looked like twins. All three were smiling. In her haste to leave, Ruth must have forgotten to take it.

Emily entered the office shaking. "I just received a call from Vince's stockbroker. It seems Vince had a secret account I didn't know about. The man said Vince was planning to buy some stock he was interested in, but the money he planned to use is gone! He seems to think Vince's assistant may have forged his signature. She handled a few earlier transactions for Vince. I didn't know anything about this until the broker just called wanting to speak with Vince. Word hasn't gotten out about Vince's death. I've delayed putting an announcement in the newspaper. I was going to ask Ruth to do it."

"How much money is missing?"

"The amount is five hundred thousand dollars! I can't believe Vince could hide that much money from me. I guess I trusted both of them and look what's happened. I'm such an old fool."

Nick got a call from his office. Success was no longer in its slip. It left sometime late yesterday. Ruth was missing along with a huge amount of money. Now the boat was missing. He'd alert the Coast Guard to be on the lookout since the boat could easily be identified. He also issued a BOLO (Be on the lookout) for a red Ford Mustang with a tan convertible top. *He'd neglected to note the license plate number. A patrol office would do that as a routine item.* Nick doubted Ruth took the boat. But, if she had an accomplice, or two young chaps who looked like twins, they might be involved. Nick had to consider possible places where one could hide a large, expensive boat. An alert to all the marinas in the Great Lakes area might help. Leaving Lake St. Clair, you had to navigate the Detroit River which dumped into Lake Erie. Going East you had a couple of islands north of Sandusky to investigate. Erie and Buffalo would constitute the maximum limit. Somewhere in that area they had to hide the boat.

"Everyone was convinced this was an accidental drowning," Nick said in the office for everyone to hear. We have a suspect in hiding who embezzled a ton of money and this isn't her first rodeo. She took an older investor in St. Louis for a bundle and fled two years ago. This is a dangerous dancer," Nick announced. *A dancer being a suspect who evades questioning.*

Two days later, Nick received a call from a duty officer in Sandusky, OH. "We've spotted your red Mustang parked at a cheap motel on the outskirts of town. We have a cruiser keeping it under surveillance. What do you want us to do?"

"I'll be there in three hours," Nick said. He'd use his

own vehicle with a red flasher on the dashboard. As a detective, Nick preferred using unmarked vehicles.

Nick made the trip in record time, located the motel and checked in with the desk clerk for a room with a direct view across from the parked Mustang. Ruth Lambert was not registered, nor was a Rita Lawson. There was a registered guest named Robin Lester. Registration for the Mustang was made to Zephyr Ltd. In Ft. Lauderdale, FL. A quick search revealed it was a used boat dealership. Perhaps the missing yacht was destined to relocate there. It was all starting to come together. Ruth, with the help of her two friends, were swindling rich people, stealing their investments and their toys.

A few hours later, Nick's phone rang. "This is Deputy Sheriff Alan Green. Are you the officer looking for that stolen boat?"

"Yes, have you located it?"

"Yes sir, it's hidden away in a small private marina on Middle Bass Island. Do you know where that is?"

"Yes, I've heard of it and I know approximately where it is. How can I get there?"

"We have a fast boat we borrow when we need it. I'll pick you up and take you there. Are you at the motel where they spotted the missing red Mustang?"

"Yes." Nick suggested they meet in front of the office.

The deputy arrived in an unmarked vehicle and

explained he was working a stakeout using his own Jeep. They drove to a local marina where a speed boat was waiting. Nick was helping to untie the craft with his back to the deputy when he was hit from behind. The blow knocked him to the floor of the boat as it sped away from the marina.

"Just stay down there until I tell you to get up," the false deputy yelled.

They were skipping across the water at a high speed. Someone else was steering the craft while the false deputy leaned down and tied Nick's hands behind him.

"Nicky, you sure have caused us a lot of undo aggravation."

A sudden kick to the ribs caused Nick to curl into a fetal position. His pistol had been taken. Nick closed his eyes and willed the pain to lessen. The false deputy's face was an older version of one of the twins in the photo Nick found at Emily's. The other twin must be at the wheel, he thought. They had set a trap, and in his haste to catch Ruth, he'd fallen into it. His hormones had overruled logic and routine. He felt stupid.

"You might be interested to know that the boat you're looking for belongs to me and my brother. Ruth sold it to us last week. We are in the process of registering it under the name, *New Start*. Pretty clever, huh? And, we already have a buyer. We just have to deliver it without being chased. And, we're about to solve that problem. Ha, ha, hah."

Suddenly the two outboard engines were idling. "Time to take a swim, Nosey Nicky." The two brothers lifted Nick up and over the side of the boat. Nick managed to catch the knot holding his wrists together on a cleat as he was being pushed overboard. The knot came loose enough for Nick to work his hands free. He rolled over on his back and tried to float. His teeth were chattering from the cold water. He lost track of time kicking and working his arms in a forced rhythm to stay afloat.

"Ahoy there, you need a lift?" Three fishermen in small boat approached.

Nick wasn't sure if they were real. Maybe he was delirious. He was waving his arms when they lifted him into their boat. "What the heck are you doing out here?" one of them asked.

Later, Nick would ask himself that same question. Danger comes in many ways, many forms, sometimes dressed in a beautiful costume smiling, seducing the senses. Ruth's image would remain seared into Nick's brain for as long as he lived. Someday...he'd find her again.

End

Dangerous Relationships

Nick Alexander's new occupation as a private investigator suited him. After 20 years with the St. Clair Shores police, he was ready for a change. Now, his specialty was doing background checks for large organizations with military contracts. Being single, he liked the freedom to travel and see new places. The Holiday Inn empire suited him and soon became his secondary office away from home. The establishment provided decent meals and a convenient bar.

He was on his second Gin and Tonic when two attractive ladies sat at the bar next to him. The blond looked over at Nick and smiled. Nick nodded a hello. A few minutes later, he overheard their laughter and mention the name McDermitt. McDermitt Furniture Manufacturing was the new client he was scheduled to see tomorrow morning.

"Excuse me, did I hear you mention McDermitt?" Nick asked.

"Yes, we work there."

"Well then, allow me to buy you ladies a drink. I have an appointment tomorrow with your human resource manager." Nick introduced himself passing his business card.

"Oh wow, a private investigator! I'm Sherry and this is my friend, Candy. We work for McDermitt. I'm the receptionist and Candy is a secretary in the marketing department. What's your interest in McDermitt?"

"As I understand it, your company has contracts to make furniture for U.S. embassies all over the world. That contract requires periodic background checks on some of your key people. That's what I do."

"I guess you'll be seeing mister Henry. He's a super guy. Everybody likes him."

"That's who I have my appointment with. Do either of you know the president, Travis McDermitt?"

"Oh yeah, Sherry knows Travis. She's his favorite hostess when we get visitors." This comment got Candy a poke in the arm.

A few awkward moments of silence followed. Nick noticed Sherry looking at her hands and smiled as if remembering something from the past. Nick didn't want to intrude on her thoughts. He thought Sherry was quite attractive and wished he could discuss McDermitt privately without her friend interrupting. Candy gave Nick a big smile. If he offered to buy another round, he was sure Candy would readily accept.

"Perhaps I'll see you tomorrow." Nick paid the tab and

left wondering what had caused the mood change. Sherry was wearing what he'd call a sad smile. If she had red hair, she could easily look like another enchanting woman Nick knew, Ruth Lambert. Ruth disappeared two years ago when Nick was still a detective investigating a drowning accident that became a homicide. Ruth became a key suspect. She still haunted his thoughts. Sherry triggered that memory.

Nick arrived promptly at 8:30. The plant was located on the south side of Cookeville, TN, halfway between Knoxville and Nashville. It took him less than ten minutes to get there from his motel. Sherry greeted him like an old friend walking him to Henry's office.

"Maybe I'll see you later," she said leaving. Nick liked the hanging suggestion.

Henry was balding and portly, wearing suspenders. His jacket was over the back of his chair. He gave Nick a solid handshake and a big smile. "You come well-recommended, Nick."

Nick and Henry spent a half hour in the office before taking a tour of the plant. The tour ended on the second floor with the executive offices. A wide stairway led from the reception area on the first floor. Purchasing, Human Resources and Sales were on the first floor. Travis McDermitt's office occupied a corner area with a double door entrance. His secretary sat outside the door as a blocker. Henry introduced Nick to Carol as Travis's personal secretary. Carol got up to shake Nick's hand with a very pleasant smile. He liked her instantly. She was his age, well put together wearing a suit and a single strand of pearls. Henry had no doubt alerted her earlier of Nick's arrival. She already knew why he was visiting.

"Carol knows everyone and everything that's going on around here. Without her my job would be much more difficult," Henry said. Carol opened the door behind her to give Nick a peek at the inner sanctum. A stone fireplace dominated one wall. Floor to ceiling windows overlooked a gathering place behind the plant. Travis's desk was twice the size of any desk Nick had ever seen. The office exuded a power image.

"Travis is in the plant, so this was a good time to show you his private digs," Carol said.

"How long have you worked here?"

"Henry and I joined the company at the same time. Travis's father started the company and he hired both of us. We inherited Travis. Travis is president, but he doesn't own the company. He's a major shareholder along with his brother who doesn't work here."

"My impression, without meeting Travis, is the man has a big ego."

"You nailed it. He's the boss and everyone here knows it. To answer your question, I've been with McDermitt for twenty years. Travis can't fire me because his father left me with some stock in the company when he retired."

"Sounds like the old man was pretty clever. You and Travis get along okay?"

"Yes and no. Sometimes things get a little hectic around here. I have Henry to vent my frustrations on. He's a gem."

"I saw a picture on the wall of a huge houseboat. Does that belong to Travis?"

"No, it actually belongs to the company. Travis uses it to entertain guests. It's been a bone of contention for a while."

At that moment, a very handsome guy appeared at the top of the stairs. Carol turned and introduced Nick to Travis McDermitt. He and Nick were the same height and build.

"I doubt that you'll find any spies working here," Travis said while shaking hands. "Did Henry give you the nickel tour?"

"Yes, very impressive. Working with Henry will be a pleasure."

"Well, let Carol here know if you need anything. She's my right arm." With that, Travis entered his office, closing the door. It was an abrupt exchange leaving Nick to feel he wasn't really important.

"He can come off as rude at times," Carol said. "He's better after lunch." It didn't take much for Nick to conclude that Carol was an important employee in the organization.

She was a good buffer for Travis with better form and manners. Big egos didn't bother Nick.

Carol's intercom buzzed, "Carol, can you break away?" It was Travis.

Carol looked apologetic. "Perhaps we can catch up later."

Nick took the stairs down to the first floor to the reception desk where Sherry was on the phone. She motioned to Nick and hung up. "Anyone offer you coffee?"

"No, I'm ready for a cup."

"Come on, I'll take you o our break area. It's Henry's favorite hangout."

"So, you met the big guy," Henry said. "Tell me what your first impression was?"

"I hate to say this, but I think he's full of himself...big time."

"Your perception is on target. I wanted to test you a little bit. And, we'll keep this conversation between us, okay?"

"Could that also include Carol?"

"Absolutely! She and I compare notes all the time."

"What's Travis's problem? Rich kid syndrome?"

"You really are perceptive. That, and the fact that he's a heavy drinker. He has mood swings, too. Nice guy one minute, angry about everything the next."

"Sounds like he might be into drugs," Nick said

"Carol and I suspect that might be it. He spends a lot of time on that houseboat partying."

"Isn't he married?"

"To an exceptionally beautiful woman who seems to put up with his nonsense. They have two really nice kids and a doting grandfather.".

"I think it was Candy who said Travis uses Sherry to help out with entertaining guests on the houseboat. How often does that happen?"

"Candy talks too much. She pretends to be Sherry's friend, but I think there's a bit of jealousy there. She'd like to be the hostess helping to entertain guests."

While Nick was talking to Henry, Carol walked into Henry's office. "I think I need a drink. Travis is in one of his moods. How about the three of us have dinner tonight. Nick needs a positive introduction into our piece of paradise."

"Good idea," Henry said. Nick nodded in agreement.

"Tell me about Travis's brother. Does he get involved with the company?" Nick asked. Carol, Henry and Nick were sitting in a booth at Dooly's Hideaway, a busy bistro on the edge of Tennessee Tech University campus. They were on their second round of drinks.

"Carlton is a few years older than Travis. He's a commercial artist, designer and owns a small advertising agency in San Francisco. He designs most of the furniture we make here. He's more like a silent partner. He and Travis have an equal number of shares in the company. Travis has tried to buy Carol's shares, but there's a stipulation forbidding that to happen. That sort of guarantees Carol will keep her job."

"What about the father? He still alive?"

"Yes, and he still holds a third of the stock to keep everyone in check. Travis wants to own the company, or at least have complete control. As it stands, he has to give his father and Carlton periodic reports as well as Carol although she already knows because she prepares the report."

'We're currently arguing about keeping the houseboat. Carlton and I agree there's no real need for that added expense. Travis wants to keep it since he's the one who uses it. Most people around here think he's the owner," Carol added.

"How often does he use it?"

"About once a month for entertaining customers when the weather is warm. Just about every weekend for his personal use, which the company pays. Big Jim is our company handyman. He does whatever Travis needs, like washing his Land Rover, cleaning the houseboat and keeping the outside landscaping looking nice."

"So, let me ask, does Sherry get paid extra for being a hostess on the houseboat?"

"Nick, that's a discussion for another time. Travis is very

partial toward Sherry for obvious reasons; she's attractive and divorced. Is Travis sleeping with her? Who knows. We can only speculate, which I prefer not to do," Henry said looking uncomfortable.

#

"Get your clothes off and get into this hot tub!" Travis ordered. Earlier, he'd planned to meet Sherry at the houseboat. Once a week get-togethers after work, were beginning to be an unpleasant chore. At first it was fun, even exciting. Travis made promises he didn't plan to keep, like promoting her into the marketing department where Candy worked, Travis used Candy a few times in the past. She was too forward, Sherry was more passive, willing to follow his orders without question.

Travis was making Sherry's car payments and giving her spending money. Nothing appeared on the payroll. He used a disposable business expense account that was never questioned.

"Travis, honey there's something we need to talk about…" Sherry slid into the hot tub facing Travis. She was worried about how he'd react to the news she was pregnant.

"Whatever it is, it can wait. I need a little attention."

"Why does it always have to be about you? If you love me, you should show some interest in me besides the obvious." It was unlike Sherry to say something like that. She'd waited too long.

"When did I ever say I loved you? I own you. You do as I say!" In the next instant he slapped her causing her head to snap sideways. Suddenly he had her by the throat. "Okay, what is it you want to tell me? Now's your chance."

"Ugh, I'm pregnant, ugh…"

"What? You been whoring around on me?" This time he punched her in the face so hard he broke her nose. Blood spurted everywhere. "I should have known. What he hell was I thinking, messing around with you? You're just a whore, and I'm not the daddy. I got fixed a long time ago," he lied.

Sherry tried to break away. Travis pulled her back grabbing her hair. He tried to hold her head under water, but she fought him, scratching his chest. Travis got out of the hot tub, went into the bathroom to attend to the bleeding scratches. Sherry waited until he was in the bathroom before climbing out, quickly drying and began to dress. Travis came out in time to see her getting dressed. He hit her in the stomach causing her to double over in pain screaming. He hit her again and she fell to the floor unconscious. Travis left her lying on the floor and poured himself another scotch straight up. He'd had several earlier and this one he felt instantly. He sat down on the edge of the bed and passed out spilling his drink.

Minutes later, Sherry regained consciousness. She found her shoes and purse. She felt dizzy and had to steady herself to walk over to the sliding door which she'd left partially open. This was the first time Travis had ever slapped her so hard. Blood ran down her chin from her broken nose making it difficult to breath. For an instant she thought about going into the kitchen, finding a knife and burying it into his still body while he was passed out. Sherry knew she needed medical attention, the pain in her abdomen made her dizzy. She knew she was bleeding internally.

Walking half bent over and holding the railing Sherry made it to her Miata convertible in the parking lot. No one was around to notice her departure. She fumbled with her keys, finally getting the engine started, hoping the noise wouldn't wake Travis. Their intimate relationship was over. It was clear now that he never loved her, only used her. She would have to move somewhere else to put some distance between them.

These were her last thoughts as she pulled over on the winding road out of the marina. Blood seeped into the seat as she fell across the shift lever and died!

#

Eli Poog watched it all happen. He was parked beside a dumpster in the shade. It was the perfect vantage point to see inside the glass sliding door of the houseboat. He'd parked in this same spot several times watching the action taking place 150 yards away. With his binoculars he could see everything going on. Poog had been stalking Sherry for over a year. Even sent her anonymous notes. He could tell she was in bad shape as she walked to her car. He waited then followed her up the long winding road leading from the Center Hill Marina to the main highway. The road required close attention since it dropped off on one side. There was no protective guardrail, just a sign indicating the speed limit was 25 MPH.

He found her car parked at an angle beside the road, the engine still running. There was no pulse. He knew she was dead. He also knew who was responsible. Her boss was going to answer for this. With no traffic coming either way, he lifted her body gently out of the Miata and laid her in his truck's bed. He took her purse and turned off the engine. When he looked down, he saw that he was covered in her blood. She was never going to be his in life, but now she was all his! He'd bury her body on his farm and talk to her whenever he pleased. No more notes.

#

Nick spent the weekend exploring nearby Nashville. The small town of Smithville just south of Center Hill Lake didn't offer much in the way of entertainment. He was tempted to ask Carol to join him. She was easy to be with, he liked her quiet manner and easy smile. She was close to Nick's age, not that it mattered. He learned from Henry that Carol was a widow, no children, led a quiet life, did some volunteer work at a homeless shelter in Cookeville. Not since the Ruth Lambert fiasco had Nick shown much interest in another woman. Sherry was cute but much younger. They would have very little in common. Carol was different from any of the other women he'd dated in the past.

Monday started with Sherry missing! Candy offered to fill in as receptionist. Henry expressed concern because she hadn't called and wasn't answering her phone.

"I know where she lives," Carol said. "We could check on her during lunch."

Nick drove and Carol sat beside him in his rental car. Sherry's house was small. One car garage, gravel drive and no sign she was there. The lawn needed some attention.

"Something is wrong, Nick. It isn't like Sherry not to show up for work. She's very reliable."

Nick suggested they check with the sheriff's office in Smithville.

"You just saved me a trip," the deputy in charge said. "Her car was found beside the road leading down to the marina. Key was still in the ignition and there was a lot of blood on the driver's seat. No evidence of an accident. We've checked all the medical centers with no hits."

"Let's check on the houseboat," Nick suggested.

A huge black man was cleaning the houseboat when they arrived. Carol recognized Big Jim and said hello. She told Nick he was a handyman at the plant.

"Mister Travis said for me to clean up a mess he made this weekend."

Blood was still evident by the sliding door because Big Jim hadn't gotten that far in his cleaning.

"I think something happened over here. Maybe you should hold up on your cleaning until the sheriff takes a look around," Nick said.

"Mister Travis ain't gonna like that."

Nick used his cellphone and the same deputy answered. Nick told him he thought some sort of accident happened on the houseboat.

"It's going to be a while, everybody is out of the office right now. Anybody hurt?"

Nick decided to wait and look around. Big Jim began running a vacuum in another room. Carol borrowed Nick's car and drove back to the office. Nick saw a big screen flat TV in the master suite. He also spotted traces of blood on the edge of the bed covers and took a few more photos with his cellphone. Inside the closet he discovered a hidden camera positioned to take a video of any activity going on within the room. That prompted him to do some additional snooping. In a lower drawer of a built-in dresser he found a stack of video tapes with dates. Nick selected a tape and inserted it into a recorder under the TV. It was a porn video staring Travis and Sherry. Nick wondered if Sherry knew about the videotaping. He kept the volume turned down so as not to alert Big Jim in the kitchen. He was glad Carol had left. No need for her to see the tape. It did confirm what Henry suspected.

"Yes sir, he's in the other room," Nick heard Big Jim talking. It was the deputy who'd just arrived. Nick quickly hid the tape in his jacket. He might need it when he confronted Travis.

Nick met the deputy once again and explained that he was a former police officer and that he'd taken a sample of the blood he found by the sliding door using his handkerchief which he handed to the deputy.

"I'm not sure we can use this. It's not something we collected; therefore, the chain of evidence won't apply here."

"Okay, take your own sample then match it with the blood you said you found on the seat of Sherry's Miata. Something happened here. You might want to treat it as a crime scene," Nick advised.

"Well now, that's gonna be up to the sheriff to decide. I'm gonna have to ask you both to leave this here houseboat…now."

Nick asked Big Jim for a lift back to the plant.

"There's a strange call for you on line one, Travis," Carol said.

"You killed her and now that's gonna cost ya, big time. I saw what happened down there at the marina. Saw it with my own eyes the way you beat her up bad," the voice said. Carol was listening in.

"Who is this?" Travis said.

"Don't interrupt me while I'm talkin. I'm a witness to you beating her so bad she bled to death. If you don't want to get arrested, you're gonna put fifty thousand dollars in a sack and leave it where I tell you. You got twenty-four hours to get the money ready. I'll tell you later where to drop it. Any funny business I'll go to the authorities, and you'll go to jail! Got that?"

"Yeah, I got that. Oh my God," Travis moaned. "Who the hell was that?"

"Travis, what on earth have you done?" Carol asked standing in the doorway.

"We had an argument and I smacked her. She left and I passed out. I swear I don't know what happened after that. I don't know where she is. That crazy coot on the phone is trying to cause trouble."

"We should call the sheriff and report this," Carol said.

"No! Don't do that. I'll handle it," Travis said. With

that, he left the office without saying where he was going. He almost stumbled going down the stairs.

#

Carol met with Nick in Henry's office. She told them about the mysterious phone call and Travis's reaction.

"I think it's time we called Carlton," Carol suggested. Henry agreed.

"Travis what's going on out there?" Carlton asked on the phone.

"Nothing you need to be concerned about. Our receptionist quit and suddenly disappeared. They say she's missing. Carol must have called you."

"Yes, and I'm glad she did. Is there more to this story I should know about?"

"I'm handling it, Carl. Carol over re-acted that's all."

Sheriff Simpson arrived at the plant and was shown to Travis's office.

"What the hell have you been up to now, Travis?"

"I had an argument with one of our employees and now I understand she's missing."

"Uh huh. This argument happened while you were on your houseboat?"

"Yeah. We were having a few drinks and things got our of hand."

"Travis, was this one of your special employees? You

know, like the ones you use as escorts once in a while. I know all about that."

"Why would that concern you Simpson? Let me remind you, I'm one of your major supporters when you campaign for re-election."

"And I've saved your bacon a few times when it could have been a serious DUI. This is different. If there's an assault charge, you could be in big trouble. Keep that in mind."

"There won't be any assault charges."

"Uh huh, and how do you know that exactly? You better level with me."

"Okay, this is just between us, turns out she's a slut, tried to hook me for getting her knocked up."

"Any truth in it?"

"No. Who knows how many guys she was sleeping with. I'm the one with big bucks and that's what she was after."

"Hmm, she's naming you as the daddy and you hit her, trying to reason with her. Is that it?"

"Pretty close. I was a little juiced at the time when she told me."

"So where did all the blood come from?"

"I might have broken her nose. She scratched me pretty good. Travis lifted his shirt to reveal the scabs on his chest. Some of that blood is probably mine."

"What time did she leave?"

"I really don't know. I passed out on the bed and she was gone when I woke up."

"You didn't attempt to follow her? We found her car up the road with a lot of blood on the seat. I think you must have worked her over pretty good."

"When you're rich, they all want your money. She was trying to blackmail me. Let's just keep that information between us, okay?"

"Travis, you're making this out to be something different from what it really is. If this woman turns up dead, you could be facing a manslaughter charge, and I wouldn't be able to help you. So, let's hope she's alive and hiding out somewhere. Covering this up won't be easy. My deputy said there was a former police officer on the boat when he got there. He gave my deputy a handkerchief with a blood sample. That could pose a problem for us."

"Crap!" What was he doing there, Travis wondered.

#

"You get the money ready?" Eli asked on the phone.

"Yes. You want to pick it up here?"

"You must think I'm stupid. Hell no, I'll tell you where to drop it. Write this down so I won't have to repeat it. There's a parking lot at exit forty-two off the Interstate. There's a trash barrel on the north end of the lot. Drop the sack in that barrel. I'll be watching, so don't come with anyone. You'll be making that drop around ten tonight, not before. Got it?"

Travis knew there wouldn't be many vehicles parked in that lot at that time of night. He thought about having Big Jim make the delivery. Then it hit him, Nick Alexander was on assignment for the company. Why not use him instead.

Travis summoned Nick to his office and closed the door as soon as he arrived. He told Carol he didn't want any calls. He was being abrupt with Carol ever since her call to Carlton.

"How you doing with the background checks? Find any spies?"

"As a matter of fact, you have one Chinese worker in shipping that has a suspicious resume that can't be verified. Henry will be giving him notice later today. My final report will be ready next week."

"Before you wrap things up, I have a personal matter to discuss. I'm not sure why you were on my houseboat the other day with Carol. I guess she invited you along when Sherry was reported missing. Big Jim thought you were snooping."

"We found some blood and I gave a sample to the deputy investigating."

"Yes, I know all about that. The sheriff was here going over the details. They are still looking for Sherry. They think she may be hiding somewhere."

"Did you tell the sheriff about your affair with Sherry?"

"There was never an affair! Where did you get that idea?"

"Those video tapes suggest something different."

"There are no tapes. Whatever you saw has since disappeared."

"This one hasn't." Nick held up the tape for Travis to see.

"That's right, you were once a cop. Wouldn't that be considered an illegal search without a warrant? Or are you trying to blackmail me?"

"Do you know where Sherry is hiding?"

"No, but I know someone who does and that's what I want to discuss with you since you are still on assignment here. This old coot knows where she is and wants fifty thousand grand. I want you to make the delivery tonight."

That sort of makes me an accomplice to your crime, Nick thought. *On the other hand, he might be able to learn more about what happened.* Nick agreed to make the delivery.

Nick remembered seeing a real estate office in Smithville, near the lake. A sign in the window offered aerial property views using a drone. They agreed on $200 for an hour's work keeping a watch on the parking lot where the drop would be made and following the suspect without being seen.

The plan worked perfectly. An old rusty pickup truck

cruised the lot several times before stopping by the trash barrel. Only two vehicles were parked in the lot, both empty. Nick was able to follow the truck keeping a good separation. The trip ended with Poog's truck pulling into a farm that needed a lot of attention. The barn beside the house looked ready to collapse. Eli Poog's name was on the mailbox. Nick parked parallel to the truck and was greeted by several barking dogs.

Poog stepped out onto the porch holding a shotgun. "Best you state your business right there, mister."

"One phone call from me to the sheriff and you'll have some explaining to do. Put the shotgun away and let's talk."

Nick entered the kitchen and sat at the table. Poog laid the shotgun against the wall. The package with the money was open on the table between them.

"Is she still alive?" Nick asked.

"I wish. He beat her real bad. She was already dead when I found her."

"What did you do with her body?"

"Buried her back behind the barn near some Dogwoods. It's nice and peaceful back there. I'm making a nice wood cross to mark the grave. I haven't finished it yet."

"How did you happen to find her?"

"I been checkin on her ever since I first laid eyes on her over a year ago. I spoke to her once in the supermarket just to hear her voice. I could tell she wasn't interested in an old farmer like me. She was the closest thing to an angel I ever saw. I knew where she lived and where she worked. Followed her to the marina and saw the whole thing happen."

"I'm going to make you a deal, mister Poog. This money Travis McDermitt gave you hush money. That means he doesn't want you talking…"

"I know what hush money means."

"Okay, here's the plan. I'm going to let you keep the money. You didn't kill Sherry, but you did hinder the sheriff's investigation…" Nick had to remind himself he was no longer in law enforcement. His involvement was minimal.

"Don't count on the sheriff for much help. He's had his hand out for a long time. He won't do anything about Travis. That's why I wanted him to know somebody out there knows his secret. I swear, I'd never hurt that lady. I would have done anything she might have asked. Too bad I couldn't save her. I've been thinking about shooting Travis. Make him really pay for what he did."

"No, you don't want to do that. I want you to write a statement and sign it about what you know and witnessed. I'll keep that statement in a safe place. Under normal circumstances, the coroner would want to dig up the body to determine the exact cause of death. Travis and the sheriff might try to implicate you."

"That's exactly what they'll try. You gonna tell 'em about all this?"

"Nope. Show me her grave."

They walked behind the barn to the fresh grave site where a bunch of wildflowers were wilting. "Stay away from Travis. Let me handle him."

Sherry's body was in a safe, peaceful place, tended to by a man who cared for her. It would serve no good purpose to move her or tell Poog's sad story.

When Nick arrived at the plant the next day, Carlton had arrived along with his father. Henry indicated that a closed-door meeting was in progress. He was guessing at the outcome; Travis was going to be replaced. He was hoping the houseboat would be sold as an unnecessary asset. And while Carol could retire, Henry was hoping she'd stay on until a new general manager was found.

"Did the money get delivered?" Henry asked.

"Yep."

"Do we know who he is?"

"Nope."

"Will we ever hear from him again?"

"Nope."

"Is Sherry in a good place?"

"I believe she is."

Sherry had been in a dangerous relationship with Travis and paid a terrible price. Now Travis would be out of the picture, but haunted by the fact that someone out there knew the truth.

The meeting ended abruptly with Travis storming out of the conference room, rushing down the stairs and out the front door. You could hear his Range Rover screeching out of the parking lot, almost hitting two parked cars. Twenty minutes later he was exiting the Interstate for the marina driving way beyond the speed limit. He turned onto the long curving road to the marina losing control. The steep drop off was across the road where they found Sherry's Miata. Quite the coincidence they both perished in such a close proximity.

End

Dangerous Consequences

Ding, ding, ding, ding. A remote crossing gate lowers with flashing lights announcing the approach of an early morning freight train. It will repeat for the 10:30 PM return. Highway 57 does not get much traffic; mostly rural vehicles like pickup trucks and field equipment.

Across the tracks on the west side is a seldom-used rest area. This is the designated meeting place for Sarah Shepherd to meet with her new client. The remote location provides the necessary privacy. Sarah arrived early, checking out the location. It made her feel uneasy. Junior level lawyers earned the boonie assignments. She had driven down from Charlotte, grabbed a sandwich at a local diner in the nearest small town of Mt. Holly where she learned there was no mountain. She had a thermos of iced tea and her laptop.

The client's name is Wilson LeFever. She was told he worked for a large chemical plant on the nearby river. His shift was supposed to end at 9:00 PM. It would take a half-hour to reach the meeting spot. He needed some extra time to throw off anyone following him. Sarah was told Wilson is a supervisor with the company in charge of quality control. His new title will soon be…whistleblower!

#

Wilson was running late. A last-minute meeting delayed him by a half hour. He pulled out of the company parking lot in his five-year-old Toyoda Corolla looking in the rearview mirror. The sudden meeting put him on alert. His supervisor was asking to see his reports for the past two weeks. He'd already seen them. Now he was asking questions.

"Are you sure these are accurate?" his boss asked.

"Positive. I always take several water samples from different locations."

"The numbers look a little higher than normal don't you think?"

"Yeah, they are. Nothing I can do about that."

"We need to show we're staying within required standards."

"What are you suggesting that I change the numbers?"

"I'm not suggesting anything, but I'll pass along something I overheard recently. The company might be looking for your replacement."

"Well, that's not going to improve the numbers."

"Don't be so sure. You get my meaning?"

Wilson got the message loud and clear. They were

watching him closely and expected him to modify the numbers to meet quality standards. The problem was getting worse, chemicals were leeching into the river. The transition pond was beginning to smell, clear evidence of a violation. A new pond was being dug farther away but it wasn't finished. Wilson was ready to quit. Maybe he'd turn in his resignation next week and look around for something else not nearby. A move meant selling his house or possibly renting it to somebody. His future was tenuous.

Sending that letter to the law firm in Charlotte might have been a mistake. He mentioned he had evidence the company was polluting the river. The law firm arranged for a local personal interview with one of their junior lawyers. Her name was Sarah Shepherd and Wilson was on his way to meet her. Wilson's mistake was stopping for gas. They were expecting him! Three men he recognized from the plant approached him while he was standing beside his truck.

"Someone doesn't like you very much, Wilson," one said.

"Yeah, we're here to deliver a message," another said.

"Get back into yer truck, we're taking a little ride," the first man said pulling out a revolver and pointing it in Wilson's direction. He would be Wilson's new passenger.

The other two would follow. It would be the last anyone saw Wilson LeFever! His resignation would not be necessary.

#

Sarah was listening to some music on her iPod when the deputy tapped on her window startling her.

"Miss, this isn't a good place to spend the night," he said.

"I'm meeting someone who appears to be late."

"Uh huh, you from North Carolina?"

"Yes sir, Charlotte."

"Let's just have a look at your license and registration while we're at it."

"For what reason? I haven't done anything wrong."

"I really don't need a reason and I don't like your attitude! Get 'em out where I can see 'em…now!"

Deputy Frank Smith wasn't used to resistance. Particularly from a young, attractive black female parked in a remote area at night with an out-of-state license plate. The scene looked suspicious. Maybe this was a drug deal he'd chanced upon. She was opening the glove box at the same time Frank was unholstering his weapon.

"I guess I should inform you I'm a lawyer and I know my rights."

That explains your sassy attitude. Allow me to inform you, you ain't in North Carolina right now. You are sitting in the middle of my jurisdiction. I think I smell something funny. You been smoking any dope lately?"

"I'm recording all this on my cellphone, just so you know."

"And I'm telling you to step out of the car!"

Sarah rolled up her window and pressed the door lock. She started to dial her phone when the deputy smashed the side window. She screamed, dropped the phone and was bent overlooking for it on the floor when the door popped open. The deputy grabbed her arm and pulled her out of the car where she tripped on the door sill and fell to her knees.

"You have no right to abuse me like this!" she cried out.

"You are about to learn an important lesson on respect for law enforcement officers." Deputy Smith bent down and snapped handcuffs on her before she could move fast enough.

"You'll lose your badge once I get through with you!"

"Threatening me won't help you."

Deputy Smith realized that he'd lost control when he pulled her out of the vehicle, and she was a lawyer, which meant he had to do some creative thinking…fast. He couldn't legally arrest her now. He could perhaps plant some dope in the trunk, but the recorded conversation would be a problem. Even though this was a remote spot, there was always a chance of being seen by a passing truck, particularly when a police cruiser was present.

Desperation was controlling the moment. The woman was still on her knees when he suddenly kicked her hard in the head. She fell over instantly. He found the keys still in the ignition, found the iPhone and popped the trunk. She weighed more than expected. He had to heave her body into the trunk forcing her legs to bend. He parked the cruiser at the far end of the rest area where it was totally dark under the trees, hiding it from the highway. He'd come back for it later. Driving her car, he headed west. Left alive, she could end his career. That wasn't going to happen. There were always consequences when people failed to show respect. That had been his mantra for a long time.

#

Nick Alexander was on assignment to do some background checks for a bank in Charlotte, NC. The bank was represented by Carlson & Partners, a small law firm in the same city.

"Your resume says you were once a detective with the police," Stu Carlson said. They were sitting in Carlson's corner office overlooking the city. "We have a situation with one of our newer employees who has gone missing. The local authorities don't seem to be doing much. Could we get you involved?"

Carlson gave Nick the few details they had. The client suddenly disappeared along with the young female lawyer they sent to interview him. The case had some dangerous implications, if the whistleblower had proof of chemical dumping. The firm should have sent two people instead of just one causing an element of guilt and poor judgement. He told Nick about the meeting details in a rural location because small towns had a unique way of learning about secret activity. Sarah wasn't answering her phone or emails. Her rental Chevy was nowhere to be found. No accident reports. Last contact was a message from Sarah at a local diner where she was eating before her late meeting. She'd already scouted the remote spot. She sounded worried.

"How long has she been missing?" Nick asked.

"It's been a week. We reported her missing the next day when we couldn't contact her. At first I thought maybe she was in an accident. We checked with all the surrounding medical facilities. Nothing. The local sheriff's office found no trace of her being at that designated area"

"What about this prospective client?"

"Apparently he's missing, too. Hasn't shown up for work. Nobody has seen him. His supervisor reports he's been acting strange lately. They were planning to fire him over poor reporting."

"So, what was this secret meeting about?"

"This guy was involved with quality control at this

chemical plant. He indicated he had proof they were dumping toxic waste into the adjoining river. That would make him an important witness in a volatile trial amounting to millions in fines. If the company suspected he was planning to blow the whistle, well anything could have happened. Our gal might have been in the wrong place at a critical time."

"That might explain why this situation hasn't gathered any traction. Maybe they had their meeting and it got interrupted."

"I must admit that did occur to me. Please be discreet while you're down there. We don't want to ignite a war over toxic waste and get the feds involved. Lawsuits should go in only one direction, not backfire."

"Okay, let's see where my investigation takes us. Having the feds involved might be the correct thing to do. They have the resources."

It took Nick four hours to drive to the site of the proposed meeting. He sat in the car and tried to imagine all the different scenarios that might have happened. He'd re-visit the site when it was dark He had to admit the place was a bit spooky. A passing train with the gates down and "ding, ding, ding, ding," reminded him of the TV series, In the Heat of the Night. It was the opening scene for the series.

Nick visited the diner in Mt. Holly where Sarah was last seen. One of the waitresses remembered Sarah.

"Very put together attractive black woman. Not someone you see around here looking that sharp. Driving a nice car, too."

"She talk to anyone?"

"Just on her cellphone. That hour we aren't busy, that's how I noticed."

"Whatcha got there?" Deputy Smith said sitting down at the counter next to Nick. The deputy reached over and took the photo Nick had been showing.

"Have you seen this woman?" Nick asked.

"Sure haven't. I'd remember a pretty face like that. Why are you looking for her, she missing or something?"

"She's a lawyer out of Charlotte who was down here to meet someone. She hasn't reported in and her firm is worried about her."

"Oh yeah, I did see something about that in the office. We haven't had any accident reports in the past week or so. Can I make a copy of that picture? Better give me your card, too. I'll holler at ya if we find something. Any reward being offered?"

"Not yet." Nick found the reward comment to be out of place.

When Nick got up to leave, the deputy followed him to his car.

"Not many places around here to visit, or to hide for that matter. You thinking maybe she was kidnapped?" the deputy said leaning against Nick's s car, taking out a stick of chewing gum.

"How many missing persons' reports do you get in a year?"

"Now that you mention it, not many. Last one was a runaway wife. We didn't bother looking for her. Old coot she was living with beat the fire out of her. Don't blame her for getting out."

Something about this casual engagement bothered Nick. This false-friendly deputy probably knew everything going on it the county. Strangers got questioned. But it was the rewards comment that Nick felt was way out of place.

"Where are you staying?" the deputy asked. "Not many good places around here."

"Haven't decided yet." Nick wasn't going to share anything more.

It was 9:00PM when Nick returned to the site by the railroad crossing. He thought the dark rest area was almost invisible from the highway. You had to know where it was, or you would pass right by it at night. Once again, he tried to imagine what might have happened if Sarah had parked here in this lonely place. Nick was in deep thought when Deputy Smith pulled in and parked next to Nick. The deputy put down his window leaning out.

"I thought I might catch you out here. This the spot where your Sarah was supposed to meet someone?"

Nick didn't recall giving out those details. He never mentioned Sarah's name but the deputy could have gotten it from the missing person report. Her name would be listed but not the exact location of her disappearance. So how would he know that?

Nick drove back to the diner hoping to catch Gladys, the same waitress he'd talked to earlier. He caught her just as her shift was ending.

"Got one last piece of peach pie. I was saving it for you in case you decided to stop by."

"Sold."

Gladys brought him a cup of coffee without his asking, put the pie in front of him and sat at the counter next to him taking off her apron. Out of habit, she was checking her hair. For Nick that was code she was interested. He'd dated his share of waitresses to recognize the body signals.

"What's Deputy Smith like? Does he spend much time hanging around here?"

"He's got a circuit he checks then he stops in for coffee and gossip. Flirts with all of us, but it doesn't mean anything. There's a rumor he's seeing some married woman who's husband is in the service overseas somewhere."

"I got the impression that he knows just about everything going on in his jurisdiction."

"You got that right. He even stopped back to ask me what all we talked about when you were here."

"I guess he's suspicious of visitors. Wants to know what they're doing here, like me."

"You got him figured out alright. More coffee?"

"How long has Smith been a deputy?"

"Long as I can remember. Let's see, yeah, he started right after his cousin got sent up for stealing cars. Almost fifteen years I guess."

"His cousin from around here?"

"Oh yeah, Scooter's been out for a few years. He inherited his daddy's hog farm. He's crazy as all get out. Frank is the only person he'll talk to."

"Do you know where the farm is?"

"Yep, you'll smell it before you get there. Stinks to high heaven!"

Gladys gave Nick directions all the while wondering why he'd want to go there. "Be careful if you're planning to visit, he doesn't want anyone coming around. He's liable to feed you some buckshot."

#

Nick spent the night at a Motel 6, had breakfast at the diner early and headed for Scooter's hog farm. Nick was glad he'd brought along his Glock pistol just in case he got into a confrontation.

The road to Scooter's place was all gravel with wire fencing on both sides. As Nick got closer to the house and barn, he saw Deputy Smith's cruiser parked at the house. This was an unexpected surprise. Nick wondered if maybe Gladys had spoken to the deputy after he left? He knew a little about small town communications systems and how that worked. Nick noticed a muddy backhoe parked beside the barn. The stink was something he'd never experienced.

Deputy Smith walked out onto the covered porch as Nick arrived. He was in uniform. His hands on his hips like he was expecting an argument. No smile this time.

"Guess you didn't see the sign, Stay Out!"

"You the designated guardian here?" Nick asked.

"I can be anything I want to be, now get out of here!" Smith yelled.

"Is he here to arrest me?" Scooter asked, coming out the door.

"Shut up and go back inside. I'll handle this."

"Why would he think I'm here to arrest him? What's he done?"

"Nothing. He's a little screwed up in the head. Doesn't like people snooping around like the sign says. You got no business here."

"I'm looking for a missing Chevy Sedan. Your cousin in there likes to steal cars…."

"I didn't steal that car! Frank gave it to me. Now go away!"

Suddenly it was High Noon at the OK Corral. Deputy

Smith was attempting to withdraw his pistol when Nick shot him in the arm. The deputy dropped his pistol and screamed, "Scoot get your shotgun."

Nick kicked the deputy's knee hard enough he went down. Nick clubbed the back of his head to put him out. He used the deputy's handcuffs to keep the deputy's hands behind his back as he lay on the porch. Nick took the deputy's pistol as an added precaution and kicked in the kitchen door where Scooter was hiding under the table.

"Don't shoot me," he cried.

On the table Nick saw what looked like a new Apple laptop open. Beside it was a recent Apple iPhone, like his. Nick took out his iPhone and dialed Sarah's number that he'd been given earlier. The iPhone on the table began to ring!

"Where is the car?"

"I dug a hole and buried it, just like Frank said to do."

"Where's the woman?"

"I don't know anything about a woman, just the car."

"Shut up!" Frank yelled, his injured arm still bleeding.

Nick dialed 911. He didn't want to be there when they dug up the missing car, afraid of what they would find in the trunk. Later, leaving the area, Nick crossed the railroad tracts a final time just as the gates were coming down behind him, lights flashing.

"Ding, ding, ding, ding." *The bells are tolling for you Sarah,* Nick whispered. The sun was out but not bright enough to erase the sad moment.

End

Dangerous Intentions

General Metals Corporation in Pittsburgh, PA won an unusual government contract to produce stainless steel struts and girders for a NASA lunar landing simulator. The structure would eventually look like a giant tinker toy structure. It would also be the largest convoy to travel on the Pennsylvania Turnpike. Langley would be the destination.

"It's a huge contract and a very hush, hush deal," Steve Morgenthaler said. "We got it through a backdoor bid."

"I can help you with the necessary background checks," Nick Alexander said. "However backdoor sounds illegal."

Nick was sitting in Steve's impressive office. Steve was president of the company. He was also the grandson of a famous billionaire in New York. Nick met Steve through a mutual friend at a gala party at the Hilton located at the famous Golden Triangle where the Ohio River meets the Allegheny and the Monongahela. It's a historical spot.

"Let me rephrase that. A well-known Air Force general was my wing commander when I was in the service. He's in charge of the project."

Nick could see a large, framed photo behind Steve's desk. It showed Steve holding a helmet kneeling in front of an F104 jet fighter.

"I guess it pays to have friends in high places."

"You got it. Let me introduce you to Terry Stevens. Terry is in charge of all our marketing and promotion. His side gig is playing drums on weekends at The Gaslight in Shadyside. The Terry Stevens Trio is pretty well-known here in Pittsburgh. Being from the Detroit area you may not have heard of them."

"While I'm here I'll check it out."

"Terry, why don't you give Nick the nickel tour of the plant." Nick had to wear a safety helmet.

"I'm not used to being around so many celebrities," Nick said.

'You'll get used to it. Our vice president of sales was a star quarterback for Pitt many years ago. He has more influential contacts than Steve and I put together. He was a big hero in his time."

"I gather Steve was, too."

"Yeah, he's got a stack of medals. Married to a very beautiful woman who also happens to be very rich. Her father owns a big chunk of Alcoa."

"Wow. Lots of money around here. You'd never know it by the looks of the plant." The plant was a left over from the

'50s. Inside it was all state-of-the-art equipment. General Metals was one of a few remaining steel mills along the river.

#

Friday night Nick made it a point to check out The Gaslight. It was an elite cocktail lounge with a large crown split between the bar area and the main room with the trio set up on a small corner stage. The well-dressed ladies seem to confirm the elite label.

Terry waved when he saw Nick standing beside the bar. All the seats were occupied. Terry whispered something to one of the waiters and suddenly Nick was shown to a small round table with a clear view of the stage and the musicians. Two attractive ladies shared the table.

"Their music is really good," Nick said to start a conversation.

"Just wait, it gets better," one lady said. No introductions.

"I didn't realize Terry was that good."

"Oh, he's better than good. Everybody loves him!"

During their break, Terry came over and joined Nick and the two ladies whom he obviously knew. He took a sip of her drink and smiled at Nick.

"Doesn't get much better than this," Terry said getting a kiss on the cheek from one of the ladies. He took another sip of her drink. Then he put his arm around her shoulders and hugged her before going back on stage. As he departed, he said to Nick, "We're just good friends."

This must be his playground, Nick decided with a little envy.

#

"Did you catch Terry's jazz session?" Steve asked. Nick was reviewing his background report in a spare office.

"Yep, I'd say Terry is quite the ladies' man."

"Oh to be a drummer. He has quite a fan club."

"Isn't he married?"

"Married to a lovely wife, Susan. She used to sing with the trio before the kids arrived."

"I'd say he's one very lucky guy," Nick said thinking about the weekend.

Steve invited Nick to join he and the vice president of sales to lunch at the country club. Terry was also invited but declined. He had a meeting somewhere.

During lunch, Nick declined a second round of drinks. This was a different group of executives than he was used to dealing with.

#

Two months later, Nick was back in Pittsburgh on another assignment. He was finished with General Metals.

However, he liked Steve and Terry and thought they might get together for lunch at the Hilton.

"If Terry is free, ask him to join us," Nick said on the phone.

"Not happening. Terry is no longer with us."

"Really? What happened?" Nick asked.

"I'll tell you when I see you."

"Terry had a habit of taking really long lunches, he wouldn't get back to the office until after two." Steve explained over lunch.

"Was there a reason?"

"Yes!"

Steve went on to tell Nick that one day there was an important meeting being held at lunch at the country club. Terry didn't show up. That annoyed Steve. Terry wasn't in the office when Steve got back. He called Terry's phone. No answer. Terry's company car was a white Pontiac station wagon so he could carry his drum equipment. It was an accommodation. All the other executives drove Buick sedans. Steve decided to check some of the local bars in the area. Not seeing Terry's car, he checked a few motels along the strip. "His station wagon was parked behind The Chandler Inn. You couldn't see it from the highway."

"He was shacking up with someone?"

"I knocked on the door and Terry opened it wearing

just a pair of boxer shorts. He was surprised to see me. I told him to be back in the office in thirty minutes. As I passed by his wagon, I spotted a silver fox fur coat on the back seat. It was my wife's silver fox that I gave her for her fiftieth birthday!"

"Oh no, What did you do?"

"When he got back to the office, I had a hard time trying to control my temper. I fired him. Took the keys to the office and his wagon along with his company credit card. Told him to leave at once. It took every ounce of restraint not to hit him."

"Did you tell him you knew about him and your wife?"

"No, I didn't want her to know that I knew. A divorce would involve A big financial loss. Betrayal is a tough thing to live with."

"Do you suppose Terry suspected you knew?"

"Maybe. Probably. Hell, I guess I don't care at this point."

"Do you think he's still seeing her?"

"Not now. She's in Italy with her parents and the kids."

# # #

A month later, Nick read an article in the Pittsburgh Post and Gazette that Terry Stevens' body was found behind a local bar, in the parking lot. His head was crushed by a brick found nearby. Witnesses in the bar saw him earlier with a beautiful lady wearing a silver fox wrap.

Nick was pretty sure he knew the killer. It was all about money.

End

Welcome to
PARADISE VALLEY
Population: 4,116

Dangerous Encounters

Zipping down the highway,
Better use the by-way,
Top down, go around,
Turn it up, hear the sound.
…Going to a party!

She's a fox,
Big boom box,
Really rocks,
Knock your socks.
…Really wants to party!

Music blaring,
Really tearing,
People staring,
She's not caring,
…She's going to a party!

The Going to a Party rap piece had Cindy's head nodding in cadence to the music. It was a perfect Friday afternoon with the top down. She was on her way to spend the weekend in Chattanooga with a girlfriend. Her divorced mother was on her way to Las Vegas, hoping to get lucky.

Cindy's 10-year-old Ford Mustang convertible with dual exhaust resonators, turned a few heads. With the music blaring, she didn't hear or notice the flashing blue lights until the deputy's cruiser pulled up beside her and motioned for her to pull over.

"Guess you didn't see the sign back there. Speed limit on the by-way is fifty-five. You were doing close to seventy," the deputy said smiling. "We need to do the license and registration review, so…get 'em out so I can see 'em." Sometimes this not-so-subtle comment worked with younger women he caught in the speed trap.

"I'm so sorry, officer I didn't see the sign. I thought the speed limit on this stretch of highway was seventy." Cindy was pulling out her wallet trying to find her driver's license, the phony license that showed her age a twenty-one when in fact she had recently turned eighteen.

"My mother is going to kill me if I get another ticket."

"Well, we might be able to work something out. That will be up to the sheriff." He called for a tow truck.

Cindy's Mustang got towed and she found herself temporarily behind bars waiting for the sheriff to arrive. She couldn't believe this was happening. The deputy took her cellphone. The only person she could call, when she finally got a chance, was her aunt Carol in Cookeville, a hundred miles from Paradise Valley. It was a pleasant-sounding name for a quaint small town with a few antique shops and an old county courthouse on the square. This was Harmon County and Sheriff Billy Hargis established all the rules. His cousin ran the towing service. The radar trap on the by-way kept him busy. Towing almost always guaranteed some storage over the weekends. The sheriff wasn't in any hurry to resolve fines with the magistrate, his uncle's brother-in-law.

Saturday night cockfights in a barn just outside of town provided the most excitement. It was also a convenient distribution center for high-grade moonshine. Stolen vehicles frequently arrived at a local chop shop providing a variety of used auto parts to local repair facilities. Sheriff Billy Hargis was aware of everything going on in his jurisdiction.

Small town corruption makes this quaint-sounding town a dangerous place to visit. Bullet holes in the welcome sign is an early clue. A run-in with the sheriff makes for a dangerous encounter! Sheriff Billy has dirt on almost everyone living in town. Some dare to joke behind his back calling him, "The Big Guy" because he stands five feet six inches tall when wearing cowboy boots with two-inch heels and a Stetson Rancher hat like the one LBJ used to wear. Inside his Ford Explorer is a two-inch cushion on the driver's side allowing him to sit tall in the saddle. He prefers to carry a large 357 Magnum pistol in place of the standard issue Glock that his deputies carry.

#

Deputy Wolfe, the arresting officer discovered Cindy had two priors for speeding. With the sheriff out of the office, she'd probably spend the weekend in the cell quietly known as, "The Honey Hole." Cindy was about to experience a nasty degrading weekend there. Sheriff Billy was single and considered female prisoners a perk for his office. There were never any follow-up investigations or reprimands. One young lawyer tried to sue the sheriff's office for a series of offenses that included rape of a prisoner in custody. The evening before the hearing, his house burned down. He moved his practice to Chattanooga and the message remained for anyone else who dared to challenge local law enforcement.

All the local residents knew about the by-way radar trap. Visitors never saw the speed limit sign because it was hidden behind tall brush and low hanging tree limbs.

Late Friday afternoon Sheriff Billy was back in the office

going through Cindy's purse. She sat opposite him in an uncomfortable chair.

"I see you practice safe sex. Are your folks aware of your activity?"

"I don't have to answer that question."

"I'll take that as a no. But it makes me wonder about you. Some kids just invite trouble. Pretty young girl like you fits that profile. Here you are speeding, not paying attention to your driving, didn't even see the deputy behind you with his flashing lights, disturbing the peace and tranquility of our little town with your loud rap crap. Makes s me wonder if you're doing drugs." Continuing to search, he found $135 in her wallet. "Do you realize this isn't enough to cover the towing and storage charges? We don't accept credit cards for fines either. You better start thinking about how you'll pay the fine."

"How much is it?"

"Considering the charges, and the fact that you have two prior tickets for speeding, that's gonna cost you four hundred and fifty dollars."

"What? I don't have that kind of money." She wouldn't be able to reach her mother in Vegas. She'd already been warned, 'one more ticket, she'd lose the car and driving privileges.'

"Seeing as I'm close friends with the magistrate, and he usually goes along with what I suggest, I'm thinking a few nights back there behind bars might help you transition into a more rational individual. Consider this little chat your preliminary hearing."

"You can't do that!" she yelled.

"Miss, you have clearly missed the point I've been trying to make. I can do whatever I want. You're the one in trouble. Behave, learn a lesson from this and maybe I'll go a little soft on you. Think about that."

#

Cindy's aunt Carol received a call from Cindy's friend in Chattanooga when Cindy didn't show up. She was worried. Carol's friend, Nick Alexander was in town visiting. Carol's company was a former client and they became close friends.

"Do you think you could look into this for me, Nick?" Nick was a former detective and had numerous contacts in law enforcement. Carol gave Nick the details on Cindy's Mustang with a complete description.

Nick started by calling all the surrounding towns between Cookeville and Chattanooga asking if Cindy's Mustang had been in an accident or stolen. He was reporting it as missing.

"Most missing vehicles eventually find their way

to Paradise Valley where they disappear," an officer in Chattanooga said. "I'd start my search there."

#

Nick saw the welcome sign…and the bullet holes. It made him wonder how friendly would a town be, with a name like Paradise Valley? He Decided to scout the town, Since it was rather small, there weren't many places a car could be parked or hidden. The areas outside of town were mostly farms. He decided to eat at a diner a block off the square. It looked like a local's hangout. The name was Frankie's Café.

"Whatcha havin', Sweetie?" Her name tag indicated Melissa. She gave Nick her late-afternoon smile which took a little effort.

"What's the special today?" Nick asked, returning the smile.

"It's the same every day, meatloaf with mashed spuds and gravy."

"Sounds good. Anyplace around here where they keep vehicles that have been in an accident?"

"Sweetie, you'd have to talk to the sheriff. He'd know, I'm sure. That doesn't mean he'll tell you. He's suspicious of strangers."

"What's he hiding?"

"If I knew that, I'd either be the mayor, or in jail." She

laughed at her own joke and poured his coffee. "Sheriff has a cousin does all the towing around here. You might want to check that out." She told him where his fenced lot was located, two blocks away.

That's where Nick found the missing Mustang, parked in the lot.

"Help you with something?" Bobby Lee asked. Bobby Lee was Sheriff Billy's nephew. He did most of the towing for his dad.

"Where can I find the owner of that red Mustang?"

"You'd best ask the sheriff."

"That's what everyone keeps saying. Is he the mayor, too?"

"Might as well be. The Big Guy knows just about everything that's going on around here. You need to check with him."

"Are you the one who towed that car?"

"Like I said, check with Sheriff Billy."

"The Big Guy," Nick repeated just to be sarcastic.

#

Nick decided to drive around making a wider circle, just to get a better feel for the area. Towns with a lot of abandoned buildings told you a lot about the local economy. He didn't see that here. Off the main street, he saw several large antique stores. Just off the by-way he found a small non-franchise motel. He'd check in with the sheriff later.

"Anything going on around here on a Saturday night?" Nick asked the motel clerk. Only three units appeared to be occupied.

"The cocks will be fighting tonight. If you're looking for some really good mountain shine, that's the place to buy it. We're a dry county."

"Thanks, good to know." Nick got directions. A place like that could tell him a bit more about this strange little town surrounded by mountains in the middle of nowhere.

Nick found the farm and saw a huge barn surrounded by a variety of pickup trucks and a few vans. He estimated at least a hundred vehicles. What came as a big surprise was a deputy in uniform directing traffic. As he approached the parking area, the deputy stopped Nick's car.

"Sorry sir, only invited guests to this event," he said.

"I was told I could buy some good moonshine out here."

"Who told you that?"

"A fella I met in town," Nick didn't want to get the clerk in trouble.

"Unless you can show me an invitation or pass, you're not allowed in."

"Okey dokey," Nick said driving away slowly. That's when he noticed a white Ford Explorer with a sheriff decal on the door parked beside the big barn.

#

Sunday morning Nick was back at Frankie's for an early breakfast. Melissa spotted him and motioned for him to sit at the counter where she was already pouring his coffee.

"Did you find what you were looking for?" she asked.

"I did, thank you."

As Nick was ordering breakfast, Sheriff Billy walked in and sat down at the counter next to Nick. "I'm sheriff Billy Hargis. I understand you been asking a few questions."

"I was planning on stopping by your office later. Didn't think anyone would be up this early."

"Guess you thought wrong."

"I do have a few questions. Everyone says to check with you...."

"That's the way it works around here."

"There's a red Mustang convertible parked in the lot with the tow truck that brought it in. I'm looking for the young lady who was driving it. She's missing. Perhaps you saw the bulletin. about it"

"Huh, you have a description of this person?"

Nick gave him Cindy Stevens' name and description. He noted the sheriff didn't write anything down.

"So, who are you and what's your interest in all this?"

Nick gave the sheriff his business card and told him Cindy's aunt was worried about her niece. He'd found the car in the impound lot.

"First of all, you got no business snooping around that lot. It's private property and I could arrest you for trespassing."

"You'd have a hard time with that."

"Think so? You don't want to get on my bad side."

"Which side would that be?" Nick asked. He heard Melissa snicker.

"Got a smart mouth on you. Tell you what, let's take a walk over to my office where I conduct all my business… in private."

"Not all your business. I saw your vehicle at the barn last night."

"Uh huh, I wondered who that was. My deputy told me someone was snooping around, trying to get in. Well mister investigator, you are in Harmon County, and I don't give a damn about who you are or where you're from. I make all the rules around here and I enforce 'em. As of now, you're under arrest for trespassing. Let's take a walk."

"Sheriff, do you mind if I finish my breakfast first?" A few customers were enjoying the spat and Sheriff Billy was getting a red face. "I know you're a big man in town and everyone seems to be afraid of you…."

"As they should be!" With that he grabbed Nick's arm and forced him to get up and leave. Nick left ten dollars on the counter and winked at Melissa. He'd need a friend to testify about this later.

"Book him for trespassing," Sheriff Billy told his deputy at the office, and lock him up!"

Sheriff, that's a misdemeanor," the deputy responded.

"I don't care. Do what I told you to do!" The deputy took Nick's wallet, cellphone, which was still on and Nick's belt. His pistol was locked in his car parked at the diner a block away.

"Bobby Lee, there's a car parked at Frankie's needs to be towed to your place. Hide it in the back. I need it done right away. Make sure everyone in the diner sees you hookin' it up."

"Do you realize what you're doing?" Nick yelled out from the back of the jail where he found Cindy in another cell. She was crying and didn't know Nick or why he was there.

#

In addition to being a waitress at Frankie's Melissa also cleaned a few houses. One of them belonged to Sheriff Billy. She had to admit the sheriff was becoming a problem for the town when it came to visitors. Three antique dealers had already complained that business was dropping off, word was getting out to avoid Paradise Valley.

Melissa had a key to Sheriff Billy's house. He had a bunch of keys hanging on the wall below a shelf in the kitchen. She found the spare key to his office and took it. She had a plan. She would wait until midnight when everything was quiet. Only one deputy would be on duty and one on patrol, probably sleeping somewhere out by the by-way. Not much activity at that hour. Her plan was to call and report a break in at a house on the edge of town. She happened to know the occupants were away. With any luck the office would be vacant for a few minutes; long enough to release Nick and possibly a young lady, if she was there as she suspected after listening to the exchange at the diner.

While still in Sheriff Billy's kitchen, she searched and found a box of rat poison in the pantry. She found an open box of cereal, poured a small portion of the poison into the box and shook it. She didn't want to kill him, just make him violently ill. That might put him on notice that someone was a threat to the Big Guy. That would drive him crazy. Maybe things would change in Harmon County, back to the peaceful little town she once knew.

The sheriff's office was locked and empty. Melissa used the extra key to open the door. The lights had been left on. She found the cell keys in the top drawer of the desk, entered the jail section and found Nick awake. Cindy woke when her cell door opened. Melissa relocked the front door after Nick and Cindy retrieved their personal items. Nick checked his phone. It was dead however, once recharged he could play the recorded conversation he'd had with the sheriff. He'd turn that over to the state police.

Melissa's car was parked on the square, close to the sheriff's office. She drove Nick and Cindy directly to Chattanooga leaving Nick's car and Cindy's Mustang at the tow lot to be retrieved later.

On the way to Chattanooga, Nick called his friend, Carol to report that he and Cindy would be in Chattanooga where she could meet them.

They were passed by a speeding ambulance, lights flashing. Melissa and her new friends didn't know the occupant in the ambulance. It was Sheriff Bill Hargis who had just finished a late snack, a bowl of cereal!

Paradise Valley was about to change.

End

Dangerous Flirtations

Greek mythology has it that beautiful creatures lured sailors to their destruction, on a rocky coast, singing and playing enchanting music.

The sudden #MeToo craze was causing Detective Ted Finley to work overtime. Sexual intimidation complaints were arriving daily, forcing him to establish some sort of priority, just to get through all the interviews quickly as possible. He knew some of the complaints were legitimate, and most of those were recent incidents more easily confirmed. Complaints about groping and indecent remarks, that happened 20 years ago, were relegated to the bottom of the pile. Yes, it probably happened, but why wait so long to make a report?

Now, it seemed like every woman he spoke with had a similar story to tell. The irony it represented wasn't lost on Ted. He'd been involved in a few scenarios in the past that almost cost him his job. Picking up a one-night stand at a bar was becoming hazardous for guys, whether single or not. He'd never had to use the dope pill method, drugging his date. That was disgusting! All his encounters and flirtations had been consensual…at least most of them had.

Barbara (last name withheld) sat on the edge of her sofa wearing a short skirt, showing a lot of leg. Ted was having difficulty concentrating, wondering if this was a tease. When she started to cry, he moved to the sofa and sat beside her. He put his arm around her shoulder, and she leaned into him, almost inviting something more. *She'd be easy prey, he thought.*

Before he left, she hinted she'd be willing to meet some time for a drink. Ted was acutely aware of the consequences. This could be the "Siren's Song" once again beckoning to him. It had happened several times in the past, costing him dearly with a divorce. He had to admit, he was attracted to vulnerable women. Being divorced he didn't have to face an angry wife. The chief agreed, women oftentimes flirted with police officers, and it was difficult to resist the temptations it posed. It was that sympathy the chief had, that saved him.

No question, Barbara was hot! She was a magnet for attention and didn't mind showing off her assets. Ted thought about calling her later, just to check on her. She claimed her ex-husband stopped by her house unexpectedly one night last week. He'd been drinking and forced himself on her. A potential case of attempted rape. However, it happened a week ago, without any evidence or witnesses. No torn clothing. She said she threw out the torn blouse. And, he hadn't forced his way into the house, she invited him inside, "out of concern for his inebriated condition. She didn't think he should be driving."

Ted wondered what it might be like to be married to an attractive flirt like Barbara? It would certainly provoke jealousy. Perhaps that was the basis for their divorce. Ted made a mental note to check the divorce records. His next stop was to visit the ex-husband, a part-time bouncer at a club just outside the city limits.

"She called me to come over," the ex said. His name was Sherman and he looked like an ex-boxer with lots of bulk.

"She claims you attempted to have sex with her and she resisted. You eventually passed out."

"This isn't the first time she's called the cops on me. Take a good look at me, detective. I could easily have my way with any woman. She was lonely and horny, so she called me. The only reason we didn't get the job done was I fell asleep and that must have pissed her off. So, she calls you. Next thing she'll do is hit me up for money to not press charges."

Ted had to agree, the ex-wife was no match for Sherman. The name seemed appropriate, thinking about a World

War Two tank. Ted made another mental note to check on past complaints.

His cellphone rang as he was driving back to the office.

"Ted, it's Barbara. I hope you don't mind that I called...."

"Is something wrong?"

"I don't feel safe. I can't explain it, but I'm scared...."

"Do you have someone you can stay with?"

"Not really. I guess I can call around to some of my friends, but then I'd have to explain, and answer nosey questions. I just don't want to do that right now."

"I understand, give me a minute to think."

"Ted, I'm sorry, I shouldn't get you involved in something like this. It's my problem. Maybe I could hire a bodyguard. Do you know anyone?"

"Look, stay put. I'm on my way to the office. I'll swing by and pick you up in about an hour. We'll have a drink and try to put something together."

"I really appreciate that, Teddy! Can I call you Teddy?"

"Oh yeah, I can be your teddy bear!" This had all the standard makings of a big fat trap. Ted wondered if Sherman was the jealous type. Would he become a problem? With 20-years of experience as a police officer, Ted knew all the danger signals of this come on, yet he wanted it to play out differently. Barbara was not someone he would ever consider marrying. Maybe they'd have a short-term affair, then it would be over. It had happened before. Eventually

he'd be too old to fool around. That's when he'd need a loving wife who didn't make too many demands on the relationship. Someone he could trust.

#

"Hey, detective, remember me, Sherman? Ted held the phone away from his ear. The man was yelling.

"A couple of months ago, wasn't it?"

"Yeah, I hear you're bangin' my ex, any truth to those rumors?"

"Since you're no longer married to Barbara, what difference does it make to you?"

"Well, see I've never really gotten over her, if you know what I mean. I keep thinking we'll get back together someday. Once upon a time, we had a good thing going."

"I don't think she sees it that way, Sherman."

"Probably not with you in the picture."

"Is that a problem for you?"

"Yeah, it is! I see your truck in her driveway. I know where you take her to eat and drink. In fact, detective, I know a lot about you, and some of your past encounters. You're a real horn dog!"

"That sounds like you are stalking, buddy. You could get into some trouble, if either of us makes a complaint."

"I don't make threats and I'm not even giving you a warning. I'm just telling you that you are messing around with the wrong person, and I might have to step in and correct the situation, at a time not of your choosing. Get my drift?"

"Sounds like a threat to me, Sherman."

"If it is, you'd be wise to move back to your old place and forget about interfering with my property."

"She's not your property!"

"She will be, once you're out of the picture."

Ted had a decision to make. Should he report the threat just made? If he did, he'd also have to reveal that he'd been living with Barbara for the past two months, exposing a personal situation that could cause a problem at work. Sherman was another problem he'd have to deal with soon. The man was dangerous! His stalking was another serious problem. If Barbara knew about it, it would add to some of her anxiety. She thought she saw him wherever they went. Until now, Ted thought she was being paranoid and hadn't taken her seriously. It was beginning to feel like a trap; the kind he promised never to make again.

End

**DETECTIVE'S DEATH
RULED AN ACCIDENT**

Ted Finley, a police detective with 20 years on the force was found dead with a broken neck at his home in Tullamore Hills. Investigators are calling it an accident. The victim was found by a fellow police officer when the victim failed to answer his phone. He was divorced, no immediate family. He was also on suspension for undisclosed issues.

Dangerous Waters

A retired homicide detective is haunted by a 15-year-old. old case, and the disappearance of a major suspect.

She looked familiar. This crazy searching had been going on for the past 15 years, ever since Ruth Lambert suddenly disappeared. In every incident, where he thought he'd seen her, it always turned out to be someone else. Nick Alexander discovered there were a lot of look-alikes.

Something about this woman he was looking at brought it all back. Nick still had her pictured in his mind: red hair, beautiful teeth, and great smile. Great body, too. She had a teasing presence that caused young men, and older guys like Nick, to take a second look. Ruth liked showing off her long legs. Most of all, she liked being around big money! She also kept dangerous company with two younger men who happened to be twin brothers. Together, they almost succeeded in killing Nick during his investigation. One brother subsequently went to prison. The other brother disappeared. The unique timing of both disappearances led Nick to believe they remained together somewhere. He thought they may have returned to Florida where Ruth said she spent most of her earlier life. She told Nick she loved being near the ocean. She loved excitement and being around rich men. Nick was an exception. He tried to provide a modicum of excitement, hoping to impress her.

Now, 15 years later, Nick could still recall all the details. He and Ruth met during a very strange homicide investigation that first appeared to be an accidental drowning. Nick was a detective then. Ruth was the victim's assistant. She provided a lot of background information about the victim's business and his clients. Nick became instantly infatuated. So much so he violated one of his personal rules not to discuss an investigation and the details. She was easy to talk to, listened carefully and made intelligent suggestions. As a result Nick used some of the opportunities just to be with her. Later, he realized that she'd just used him and he felt foolish. He discovered Ruth had a shady past that included hanging with some big-time drug dealers. Ruth's sudden disappearance made her a prime suspect. Once in a while she appeared in his dreams.

The cruise ship Nick had just left was a long overdue vacation. Here he was in Nassau, in the Bahamas, walking through the famous Straw Market when he saw her! She was wearing a large straw hat, oversized sunglasses and a flowered sun dress.

She'd taken off her sunglasses to examine a straw handbag. That was the precise moment Nick noticed her. Nick knew instantly that it was her. She still looked great. She must have sensed someone was looking at her because when she looked up, she looked directly at Nick who was standing 30 feet away. After a brief moment she smiled recognizing him. It was all the confirmation he needed. It ended when he was jostled by a group of passing tourists.

And suddenly she disappeared into the crowd. The big straw hat hid most of her hair, but enough still showed to allow him to see it was still red. It was definitely Ruth.

Nick walked through the marketplace to Bay Street checking both sides of the busy street. He knew she could have ducked into any of the dozens of shops, so he progressed slowly, looking left and right. Traffic was heavy, the street was crowded with tourists from three cruise ships in port at the same time. Nick's original destination was The Atlantis on Paradise Island, to spend a few hours in the casino.

Nick didn't see any passengers on his cruise ship who looked like Ruth. He would have noticed. Perhaps she was on one of the other ships, or she might be staying at The Atlantis.

It was a six-dollar shared cab ride to The Atlantis, crossing a small canal to Paradise Island. Nick marveled at the towering structure. It looked exactly like the TV commercials. Nick found the security office near the entrance.

"Hey, do I know you? You look familiar," one of the older security guys asked. He was sitting at a monitor that scanned the lobby entrance. Other monitors scanned the casino, the slots and table action.

"Name's Nick Alexander. You ever spend time in the Detroit area?" The man looked familiar. He was perhaps a few years younger than Nick's 60, but not as fit.

"That's it! Yeah, I knew I'd seen you before. I'm Lou spencer. I worked Bloomfield Hills P.D. a long time ago, mostly patrol. Everything okay?"

"Uh huh, I spent a lot of time on Woodward Avenue up around Long Lake Road. Do you remember the Fox and Hounds?" It was a famous restaurant that Nick had visited a few times, the last time with Ruth.

"Do I? I used to get a couple of DUIs a week coming out of that place. Lee Iacocca used to hold court there. In fact a lot of auto execs had two-hour lunches there."

"Lou, maybe you could help me out. I'm looking for somebody who may be staying here. If you've seen her, you'd remember her; gorgeous red head, probably in her mid-fifties now, but looks younger. Very sexy! Today when I saw her she was wearing an orange flowered sundress, big floppy straw hat and big sunglasses. Looks like a movie star. Have you seen anyone like that?"

"Nick, we get thousands of visitors coming here every day. I haven't noticed anyone by that description, but it doesn't mean she's not here. Where are you staying?" Lee asked.

"That's another problem. I'm only here for the day. I'm on a cruise ship. Next stop is Saint Thomas. Let me give you my cellphone number, just in case you do see her."

"If she's not on one of the cruise ships, and if she's not staying here, she could be at one of the resorts or one of the many yachts here. Guys at the marinas would remember someone like that. Come on, let me treat you to a great lunch, on the house."

Nick wasn't interested in cop talk, but sometimes you had to suffer indulgences to get the help you needed. The clock was ticking, and he had a lot of checking to do.

Over lunch Lou asked, "You still carry a shield?"

"Nope, I retired years ago. I started a private investigations business doing background checks for companies with government contracts."

"Sounds dull. No excitement doing computer stuff."

"That's pretty much what it was. The money was good, I traveled a lot. While traveling to middle Tennessee, I met a woman I really liked. She was a widow and also a client, then she became more than that. We got married and life was a whole lot nicer for both of us. She died of cancer two years ago. That's when I sold the business and officially retired." *Two years ago was the saddest day of his life.*

"Losing a mate really sucks. So where are you living now?"

"I moved from middle Tennessee to Vero Beach last year."

"Is the fishing any good over there?" Lou asked.

"I heard it is. I stopped fishing years ago when I had a very unpleasant incident that soured me on it forever." Nick didn't want to explain about his swimming in the ocean with sharks.

"I guess I won't go there then. So, what's up with this red head? She an old girlfriend?"

"She could have been, but there was a lot of competition. There aren't too many in my past that could make me do foolish things. She was one of those who mastered it into an art form." This was the first time Nick had ever made such an admission.

"She really suckered you, huh?"

"To the extent that you never forget! This is the closest I've come to finding her in fifteen years. And I wasn't looking for her today. I glanced over and there she was."

"Are you really sure you want to find her, Nick?"

It was a hell of a good question. One he should have asked himself years ago.

#

Nick was surprised at how many marinas there were on the island. Lots of big yachts and super big yachts. He hired a taxi, and had it wait while he talked to various marina workers. Nobody reported seeing her.

"Mostly blonds around here," one worker said.

After three hours of searching, Nick finally got lucky. One charter boat helper thought he'd seen someone that fit Nick's description.

"Last week I saw this beautiful red head sunbathing on one of the bigger yachts at the end of the marina. She wasn't exactly naked, but almost. Just had the bottom half of a bikini on and a pair of sunglasses. She didn't seem to mind showing that nice pair of ta tas."

This sounded like it could be Ruth. Nick couldn't get past the locked gate to that private section where the larger yachts enjoyed complete privacy from the outside world. He was able to learn the name of the yacht, Ben There. It was out of Fort Lauderdale. That was all he was able to learn, but it was enough to follow up on later.

Nick was so occupied in his quest to find Ruth; he'd lost track of time. His ship was departing exactly at 5:00 PM. It was now 5:35 and he'd missed the boat!

Fortunately, Nick had the taxi waiting. He had the driver take him across the island to the airport. He instructed the driver to by-pass the terminal and drive to the opposite end of the field to the General Aviation facility. A few twin and single engine aircraft were parked outside. Also a few private jets.

"Any charter operators around?" Nick asked the man at the reception desk.

"You see dat guy out der wit da brown shirt? He be by dat Cessna tail dragger. He sometimes do some work," the man said pointing out to the tarmac.

"Okay if I go out and talk with him?" Nick asked.

"Sure. Just don't go out on da runway. Dat's not so good maybe."

Nick could see the man was untying the ropes that kept the wings connected to iron rings in the cement. He estimated the pilot to be in his late 30s with a deep tan and bleached blond long hair wearing aviator-type sunglasses. He nodded to Nick as he approached.

"You interested in taking a charter flight?" Nick asked.

"Depends on where, and what I'm taking."

"I just missed my cruise ship's departure. Its next stop will be in Saint Thomas. Can you fly me there?"

"Maybe. I'm heading in that direction, but I got a stop to make first. I got to drop off some supplies for a friend of mine."

"How much? Nick asked hoping he had enough money.

"Two hundred ought to do it. That will pay for my gas."

"How soon do you plan to leave?"

"Tell you what, go inside and take a quick whiz. When you come back out here, I'll have everything ready to go. Did I mention I don't take plastic, and I don't take checks. Is that a problem?"

"No, I'll see you in a few." Nick thought the restroom visit was a good idea. He had enough cash because he'd planned on spending time at the casino. This seemed to be his only option.

He'd check up on the yacht named Ben There when he got back to the mainland. Nothing else he could do, unless he wanted to camp out in Nassau for the rest of the week without a change of clothes. All his stuff including his passport was on the ship.

Nick knew a little about small planes. He'd flown before, but never over water! This was a single engine aircraft, high wing with four seats and a tail wheel. Looking over the nose was difficult while they were taxiing on the ground. Once they were airborne, Nick could see for 20 miles. He could see different shades of blue and green water. He realized that the island they'd just left wasn't all that large, even though it was the capital.

"Here, put this on," the pilot said, handing Nick an orange life vest.

"I sure hope I won't need it," Nick replied. The island was quickly disappearing behind them and all that remained was a hazy horizon and a lot of Atlantic Ocean. He could spot a few boats in the water below, one was a cruise ship, maybe his. Another was a cargo ship going in the same direction.

"What happens if the engine quits?" Nick asked. He was feeling a bit nervous with all that water below.

"We get wet. We'll glide for a little while, not long enough to get us to any land. What most guys do in that type of predicament is to find a ship and head for it. That way, once we hit the water, we get out and start swimming toward the boat. The closer we get, the less distance we have to swim."

"What about sharks?"

"Well, they're out there, of course. Try not to let them bite you,"

Nick was trying to decide if the pilot was joking. His one adventure in the ocean with sharks was enough.

"Did you file a flight plan?"

"Every departure is required to file a flight plan. You tell 'em where you're going, how many people are on board and how long you estimate the flight will take to get there."

"And you told them all that, right?" Nick was a little suspicious because he hadn't been away from the pilot more than five minutes, and he hadn't heard any of this mentioned over the radio.

"Yeah, pretty much. Guys in the tower know me and the weather isn't a factor today."

"And they know where we're going?"

"I make this trip all the time, it's no big deal." His comment wasn't reassuring or a confirmation.

"It's a little island with a short landing strip. Depending on the wind, it can be a little tricky getting in there. That's why I fly this rig, it's a one-eighty and it can land on an eight-hundred-foot runway, it's better than most small planes for tight places."

"How long is the landing strip where we are going?"

"Oh, it's close to fifteen hundred feet, give or take."

"And who owns the island?"

"Well, I'm not exactly sure who officially owns it, but I think it's a group of guys who charter out for prize fish like Marlins. Sometimes they stop there for additional supplies. I drop off what they need and they pick it up when they come in. There's a small cove that works out nicely for them. It protects them whenever a storm pops up. It's all primitive. You wouldn't want to spend a week there. There's no electricity or running water. No communications, either."

Nick decided not to ask any more questions. The supplies thing bothered him. The first thing he thought about was drugs. If that was it, then the pilot, along with his friends were criminals, dangerous criminals!

Nick had some experience with drug dealers when he was still a cop, wearing a badge and carrying a weapon. Those days were long past. Now, he was just a civilian in a strange part of the world, where law and order was casually enforced. Drugs were known to be part of the economy. And, his gun was locked away at his condo in Vero Beach. In this awkward situation, it wouldn't be much help.

"We'll be there in another thirty minutes. Just relax, everything is okay up here. We're doing close to one hundred and forty miles an hour; we are level at eight thousand feet and we have plenty of gas. This particular model is equipped with long-range fuel tanks because many of these island stops don't have fueling facilities."

"Ever run into any modern-day pirates?" Nick asked.

"They are definitely out there. I've heard some gruesome tales. Not sure if they're true or not, but you never want to get involved with them. They steal and they kill. They never take hostages or ask for ransom. Drug dealers steer clear of them, unless they want to buy one of their stolen boats."

That was enough information. His pilot did seem to be well-informed about details. He knew what was going on. Yes, these were dangerous waters they were flying over!

The island was directly ahead at the twelve o'clock position. It looked like a small rock jutting out of the water. As they got closer, Nick saw a few trees and lots of rock. He saw the small cove the pilot mentioned and a short expanse of beach. The pilot circled the island while lowering the flaps and reducing power for their descent. Nick did not want to distract his pilot, so he remained quiet, yet tense. This a new experience for him.

Nick saw the landing strip a few seconds before they touched down. He never saw it from the air when they were circling. It wasn't a blacktop strip, it was stone and gravel and looked like the surrounding area. They bounced and rolled. Just before they stopped, Nick heard a loud pop as the aircraft veered sharply to the left and stopped at a leaning angle.

"Damn, we blew a tire!" the pilot said pounding on the control wheel.

"Do you have a spare?"

"No, there is no spare, and there are no mechanics. We're stuck here until one of the boats arrives. I can't call anyone from here, either. Were you ever a boy scout?"

"As a matter of fact, I was. Not sure how that is going to help us." Nick started unstrapping his life vest and seatbelt harness. It could have worse, he thought.

#

"So, can we use the radio to call for help?"

"We could if we were still at eight thousand feet, but we don't have any range here on the ground."

"Isn't there an emergency beacon on the plane, like when they crash?"

"Yes, its an orange box behind the baggage compartment. It goes off automatically when there is a sudden impact, just like air bags on a vehicle."

"Can it be operated manually? Like when you need help, but it isn't actually a crash?"

"Yeah, there's a switch you can turn on and it sends out a distress signal that gets picked up by high-flying aircraft overhead. We're not in an area where commercial aircraft fly."

"Why not switch on the beacon? Somebody might pick it up."

"Because we don't want anyone to know we're here. Come on, you can give me a hand unloading the cargo."

The cargo consisted of four rectangular plastic storage bins, the type people use in their garage to store tarps, hoses and used cans of paint. Two storage units were in the baggage area and two were on the back seat. They were heavy. Nick and the pilot, who finally introduced himself as Fred, carried a container each. They walked along a defined path through a rocky slope where Nick could make out a small shelter with a protruding deck. It took three trips to unload everything. The last trip involved carrying cases of bottled water in gallon jugs.

Nick had more questions but was afraid of the answers.

Fred might have lied, but it seemed obvious to Nick that this was a drop-off and pick-up spot for drug traffickers.

The shelter was one open room with the front opening onto the deck. There were several window openings without any glass, allowing a breeze to come through. Nick noticed a rusting LP tank connected to a one-burner device that looked like a hot plate. There was a cabinet, and several rolled up straw mats. The only welcomed item was a rope hammock. Yes indeed, it was primitive!

Fred said, "It keeps the rain from soaking you and provides shade from the sun, that's about all. It ain't the Hilton."

"How long do you suppose we'll be here before anyone comes by?" Nick asked.

"Couple of hours. If anyone saw us circling the island, they'll investigate. There were a few small boats out on the horizon."

Fred left all the bottled water inside the shelter. He moved the storage units from the deck, carrying them to the back and pushing them under the shelter, covering that area with pine straw. Anyone looking would find them easily enough, Nick thought. He was tempted to lift one of the lids and look inside. All four units seemed to weigh the same.

"Want something to eat?" Fred asked.

"Sure, what's on the menu?"

"Well, we got canned beans, or you can have canned beans, which do you prefer?"

"Right now, I can handle beans," Nick said smiling. It had been a few hours since he had lunch with Lou.

Nick watched Fred open the cabinet and take out a large can of baked beans. He used a can opener, the type the Army used with C-rations. Fred pulled out an unwashed quart-sized pan and put it on the single burner. He opened the valve on the LP tank, struck a match and began heating their meal.

"I got a couple of plastic spoons in there," Fred said. Nick was wondering how they would take turns eating out of the pan. Boy scouts were better prepared, he thought.

"I've got an open jug of water, but don't drink too much, in case we should be here longer than expected." It was supposed to be a joke.

Fred laughed when Nick showed surprise, they must have carried at least three dozen gallon jugs of water. That should last a long time. He doubted he could last a week just eating baked beans and drinking water. He didn't see any fishing gear. Fish would be a good alternative to beans.

Just as the sun was setting, Nick heard a boat's engine. It was getting louder, so help was on the way. Fred found a pair of binoculars on the shelf that Nick missed seeing. Fred focused on the approaching craft.

"Okay, here's what we're going to do. That will be my

client arriving. They're a bad bunch of guys and they won't be happy to see you here. You hide behind some of those rocks behind the shed. Keep out of sight. Don't come out until after they're gone. They won't be here very long."

"Are you going to ask them to radio for some help?"

"Not these guys. I've got one storage unit for them to pick up and they'll be gone in a few minutes. I don't want them to know anything about a blown tire, or that we need help."

Nick watched as Fred carried a storage unit down a different path toward the cove, about a hundred yards away. The fishing boat had a spotting tower and down riggers. It was gliding slowly into the cove. Nick could make out four people, all wearing ball caps. Two were waving to Fred.

"Hey Freddie, how's it goin' guy?" one yelled.

"Same as always, just hangin' onto the edge," Fred replied.

"And you got our stuff I see." They dropped an anchor and one of the men jumped off into knee-deep water wading toward Fred, taking the storage unit and handing it up to a man waiting on the boat. Nick couldn't make out a name of the boat. It looked like thousands he'd seen in various marinas. He guessed it was about 38 feet in length. It looked sleek, one of the newer designs.

Then he heard it. The blast was loud! It sounded like a

shotgun. Nick saw Fred slump to his knees then fall forward into the shallow water. He didn't scream. The man still on deck, who took the storage unit was now holding the gun. He put it down and jumped off the boat, joining the man already wet. They waded ashore, leaving the other two men on the boat.

"Let's see how much product he's got hidden up there in that shack," one of them said.

Nick crouched lower. They were coming up the sandy path. Now he knew why Fred had cautioned him to hide. These were drug traffickers and stone-cold killers. They stepped onto the deck, searched the cabinet then walked around to the back of the shelter. They discovered the other three containers quickly.

"Well, lookie what we found! One yelled. "Tell those guys to come up her and give us a hand."

Nick held his breath. It definitely wasn't a good time for the beans to start working in his digestive system and give away his hiding spot. It was getting dark which helped to hide his position. If asked, he couldn't identify any of the men. They all looked alike wearing cut-offs and white tees. They were just shadows and voices moving about. No accent.

Nick didn't come out from hiding until he heard the engine start. The boat was reversing out of the small cove, where Fred's body was still floating, waiting for a hungry shark. There was a time when that body could have been Nick's. It was the source of many bad dreams. Now he was seeing it in real time.

#

Nick thought about the movie he'd seen, starring Tom Hanks, who was stranded on an island after the plane he was on crashed. Then he reminded himself that every time he thought about Ruth, something dangerous seemed to happen. If not for her, he'd be on that cruise ship eating a delicious meal with a glass of wine. Later, he'd watch a floor show. Now, he was a modern-day Robinson Caruso, stranded on a deserted island, with lots of fresh water, and lots of beans!

It was too dark to take the path back to the Cessna 180 with a flat tire. He'd wait until morning to search for that emergency beacon. He would search for a flashlight and hope to find a map and anything else he could use. He crawled into the hammock and tried unsuccessfully to sleep. It was dark and very quiet. Thousands of bright stars filled the sky. He could hear gentle waves crash upon rocks and the small sandy beach below. Under other circumstances it would be a pleasant, soothing sound. Finally he surrendered to his waiting dreams.

Nick was always a coffee-first thing in the morning person and there was no coffee, just water, lots of water the men didn't take. He was going to pass on the beans until it was absolutely necessary. He hummed an old tune from the past, *Twenty-six miles across the sea....* He'd already passed a lot of gas and was thankful it didn't happen when the visitors were there searching the shelter. It would have given away his location and he'd be out there somewhere with Fred. He'd searched for Fred's body when he woke. There was nothing to find. *Santa Catalina is waiting for me....*

It was a new day, he was alive and therefore optimistic that he'd be rescued eventually. He found the ELT, emergency locator beacon and flipped the switch to the on position. He sat in the cockpit, turned on the ignition switch, turned on the top radio and called, "Mayday, mayday, I need help." He repeated the message several times before turning everything off. He found a first aid kit under the seat, but no flashlight. In a map pocket on the back side of the pilot's seat, Nick found Fred's wallet. He found $2,200 and learned Fred's real name was Ronald Frederick Nelson. He had a Bahamian driver's license with a Nassau address. Nick would notify the authorities of his death when he had a chance.

Next project was to scour the small island to search for driftwood to build a fire, one that might draw enough attention from a passing boat. The question was, would it be a repeat performance like the one that ended Fred's charter career? Gathering wood gave him a reason to keep busy and inspect his surroundings. If he ever got off this island, he'd have an interesting story to tell, even if it sounded unbelievable. It took less than an hour to circle the entire island. He wondered what it would be like during a hurricane.

This was a remote bit of rock sticking out of the water and didn't offer much in the way of protection against the elements. There was a constant breeze and little else. While exploring the perimeter of the island, Nick kept looking for Fred's body, not sure he wanted to find the partial remains.

# # #

Nick appreciated the shelter with a hot sun overhead. He was taking a mid-day siesta, enjoying the constant breeze when he heard a voice yell, "Ahoy, anyone here?" At first, Nick thought he was dreaming again. He hadn't heard the boat come into the cove because it was a sailboat, a large sailboat. Two people in a rubber dingy were rowing to the beach. One of them was a young woman. They didn't look like drug dealers, so Nick walked down the path to meet them.

"Hello, and thank goodness you came," Nick said.

"Was that your emergency signal we heard?" the man asked.

"Yes! I'm glad you picked it up."

When he took off his cap, Nick could see his partially

bald head. The hair on his chest was white along with his beard. Nick guessed he was in his late 50s. He was slightly built, around five feet seven inches tall and had a British accent. The woman was younger, maybe early 30s with bleached blond hair, slim build and very pink from too much sun.

Nick helped them pull the dingy ashore and introduced himself. "I'm Nick Alexander and I've been stranded her for the past two days. The chartered plane I was on blew a tire when we landed." Nick went on to explain what happened.

"There are drug dealers everywhere in these waters and pirates, too. You can't be too careful. Name's Timothy Longworthy, this is my first mate, Pam. We met in Gibraltar," Tim said.

"I was on holiday," Pam added. She also had a British accent.

Nick wasn't sure any of that mattered, but he listened to be polite. "So where are you headed?"

"We're on our way to Nassau, would that help you? Our last stop was Antiqua."

"I left from Nassau. Right now, anyplace other than this island would be wonderful. He needed something good to eat and a shower. He wasn't used to living in his clothes for more than a day. "Do you mind if I tag along?"

"Nonsense, no trouble at all." Tim said. "Anything you need to bring with you?"

"The only thing you might be able to use is some water. There are several gallons in the shelter."

"Excellent! We can always use more drinking water."

"Do you by any chance have a camera?" Nick wanted to take a picture of the plane to help explain his experience later.

"Sure thing. I've taken hundreds of photos since I began this trip two months ago."

On the way to Nassau, Tim explained the boat was a 1983, 45-foot sloop made by Morgan. A very sought-after sailboat. It was a Nelson Marek designed craft built for ocean sailing. Tim said he bought it from the original owner ten years ago. He'd sailed from England down the coast to Portugal, then onto Gibraltar, where he met Pam. She was a schoolteacher, single and looking for some adventure.

"My previous mate left me in Portugal for a much younger bloke. While I can sail this ship by myself, it's much easier when you have a second person helping you."

Nick wondered how much helping out Pam actually did? She had fair skin turned pink. Nick could tell she was a flirt by the way she smiled at him and winked. He hoped she wouldn't become a problem on the way to Nassau. Nick planned to ask Lou at the casino for a little help with reporting Fred's murder. Then he'd get a commercial flight back to Fort Lauderdale, meet his cruise ship, gather his luggage and head home. Hopefully without any more incidents.

Ruth, who was the object of many dreams, could become a search project for another day, He'd chased that ghost for 15 years, so another few months wouldn't make much difference. Lou's question, "Are you sure you really want to find her?" made Nick dig deep into the hidden compartments of his brain and to ponder if it was really worth the effort. Right now, the song in his head continued, *"...Santa Catalina, the island of romance."*

The three of them loaded the water, took pictures of the plane. Then Tim and Pam posed while Nick took a photo of them with the sailboat in the background. Once on board, Nick saw his face in the mirror and realized how grizzly he looked. Tim offered a razor and Pam offered to shave him. Nick became aware of how close Pam stood beside him, rubbing against him. Tim was topside and they were alone.

"I'll bet you have lots of interesting stories to tell," she said. Nick had mentioned earlier, over a warm beer, that he'd been a detective years ago in another life. It wasn't meant to impress anyone, but it must have intrigued Pam. There was a time when Nick was still working as a detective that he might have encouraged a young woman like Pam. There were a few in his past; faces remembered; names forgotten. He and Tim were close to the same age and Pam was way too young to be a close companion for either of them. The age difference prohibited a meaningful relationship. Nick's priority was to get back to Nassau, not to compete for this young woman's affection.

Nick said, "I'm old enough to be your father."

"What does that mean? You prefer older women?"

"I prefer women with whom I have something in common. Older women like the same music I like. They remember earlier times that we've both lived through...."

"Oh rubbish! I think older men are afraid of younger women because we have more stamina for sex."

"Maybe that's it," It was all he could think of for a reasonable response. Agree and change the subject, he thought. He was trapped. He couldn't get out and walk to Nassau.

They sat outside in the cockpit enjoying a glass of wine. There was a steady breeze and a beautiful sunset. Nick almost felt human again. The craft handled well. Nick liked it.

"We'll use our running lights, but we must keep a sharp eye out for other vessels," Tim warned. "Pam can take the early watch, and it's up to you, Nick which watch you're up for. We'll do four hours each. That way you can get some sleep. Autopilot was operating.

Nick agreed to the second watch. He worried about Pam, she was on her third glass of wine. Nick stopped after his second. He slept on a sofa-like bench below in the lounge area. He liked the gentle motion of the boat, but it was still way too small to eliminate any apprehension. Small boats on large bodies of water did not make him feel comfortable. The wine helped him fall asleep.

Nick woke in total darkness. A luminous nautical clock on the wall indicated it was 12:30 AM. Pam should have alerted him it was his watch a half hour ago. Instead, she let him sleep. As he climbed the steps, opening the hatch, he discovered the reason, Pam was asleep! The autopilot was maintaining a steady course. Pam was slouched to one side. Nick pushed her and she woke, startled.

"I guess I must have dozed off," she said.

"A little too much wine can do that," Nick answered.

"Nickie, are you reprimanding me?"

"Just stating a fact. Good thing no pirates approached."

"You are reprimanding me! If you promise not to say anything to Timmy, I'll make it up to you. It's a bit chilly to get naked, but we should warm up soon enough."

"I don't think that's a good idea. I'm a guest on Tim's boat after all." Pam was cute, and available, but not his type.

"He doesn't have to know. I doubt he'd really care. Don't you want to have a little fun?" She curled next to Nick allowing her hand to fall on his thigh.

Nick pushed her away and stood to stretch. He scanned

the dark background. A sliver of moon was out, enough light for him to see an approaching vessel without running lights! Nick told Pam to wake Tim while he shut off the running lights and changed course.

"I think we have unwanted company coming."

#

Tim came topside carrying a hunting rifle with a scope. He showed Nick how to operate the spotlight without turning it on.

"We have to wait until they get closer, turn on the spot and give them a few shots as a warning that we're on to them," Tim said. "Good thing you were alert." Another half hour of sleep and they might have been surprised by an unwanted intruder, Nick thought. Regardless, they were in trouble. Nick suggested that Tim use the radio to ask for help, before the gap closed completely.

By the time Tim re-emerged, the shadowing vessel seemed to take a different course away from them.

"They must have been monitoring our transmission," Tim said.

Fifteen minutes passed when they heard a helicopter approaching. Tim turned on the running lights and went below to answer the radio. They were asking about their situation. Another minute they were hovering overhead, shining a light down on them. Nick and Pam waved. Nick considered the whole event as a moment of good luck.

Pam gave Nick a furtive look, hoping he wouldn't say anything about her falling asleep.

The Bahamian Coast Guard wanted a full report on the incident once they were anchored in the harbor. They were taken ashore to be interrogated. The officials examined Tim's and Pam's passports and asked Nick for his. He explained everything that had happened so far, nothing about the search for Ruth. He said Lou, at the Atlantis could confirm part of his visit, and someone at the general aviation center could confirm his recent departure with Fred. He showed the digital photos of the plane listing to one side on the runway.

Two hours later, Nick was repeating the lengthy explanation to a police inspector who held the photo of the plane and was taking notes.

"You say the pilot was shot and left in the water. Later, when you went down to the beach, you said you didn't see his body in the water, is that correct?" the inspector asked.

"Yes, I looked, but didn't see any trace of him."

"So, you don't know if he was dead, or not."

"I think you can safely assume he's dead. He was floating face down and wasn't moving after they shot him at close range."

"You saw all that, but you could not see a name on the boat"

It went on like that for another hour. Nick had to wait while they; checked with the cruise line about a missing passenger named Nick Alexander not returning to the ship.

"Was it your plan to rendezvous with someone on the island?"

"No, the pilot said he had one stop to make on the way to Saint Thomas."

"So, you say. There is no filed flight plan."

"I took his word that he filed. I don't know much about aviation procedures."

"Why not just buy a ticket on a commercial flight?"

"I thought I might get there quicker this way."

"I find your sense of logic wanting, Mister Nick Alexander, former police officer and detective now retired. In your previous employment, did you ever encounter drug traffickers?"

"Yes, I found them to be a dangerous group."

"They are even more dangerous here in the islands. You are fortunate they didn't find you while searching."

"I'm glad they didn't search the entire island. They just looked around by the shelter and found some storage units hidden beneath it. They didn't know I was there, or they would have shot me as well and I wouldn't be here reporting the incident."

"It is unfortunate the pilot's body wasn't found. And, I wish I had the name of that boat you saw. As it stands, we only have your word for this fantastic series of tragic events."

"I wish I could be more helpful."

"Tell me once again, how all this happened, that you missed your cruise ship's departure. I'm curious about that."

"I was making inquiries about someone I once knew and thought they might be staying here at one of the marinas. I also checked with security at The Atlantis where I happened to meet a former police acquaintance. He's working security there." Nick had been over this twice already and was trying not to be annoyed. He knew somebody was already checking the story for confirmation.

"We can get you through security at the terminal here, but I strongly suggest you take a shower and find something decent to wear before you depart. Otherwise, I suspect you will be vigorously questioned again upon entering the United States," the inspector said. He was smiling for the first time.

Nick knew he looked like a homeless person. He needed to change his appearance. Being reminded of that fact gave it first priority. Tim stuck around to help corroborate his statements. They left Pan on the boat.

"She's a bit of a flirt, don't you think?" Tim asked.

"She's young and single, looking for some fun and

adventure. I doubt either you or I could hold her attention very long," Nick said. Tim nodded in agreement.

"Well, it was fun for a few weeks, but to tell you the truth, I think I'll look around for another mate. Perhaps someone a bit older." Nick had to agree.

Back at The Atlantis, Nick used Lou's apartment to shower, shave and borrow some clothes before heading to the airport. Lou drove him and waited until his flight was boarding.

"If you visit Florida anytime in the future, look me up," Nick said giving Lou his address.

"I'll keep my eye out for your red head, Lou said waving goodbye.

In Fort Lauderdale, Nick picked up his car. The cruise ship wasn't due back in port for another day, so he had to wait around and kill some time. He stopped by the local Coast Guard station to inquire about Ben There.

"She's usually docked over at Pier Sixyt-Six. We show the owner as Majestic Enterprises in the Cayman Islands, but it's also registered here. Benjamin Sigler is the listed agent. He's probably the owner as well, considering the ship's name."

"Any idea when it will be back here?"

"No idea. You said you saw it in Nassau?"

"Yes, but not up close." Nick surmised it would take a small fortune to maintain a super yacht like that. Maybe a regular crew of five or six people, dock fees, fuel, food and lots of expensive booze. A company-owned yacht could write off most of those costs as business expenses. An individual had to have big bucks to sustain that kind of lifestyle. If Ruth had ideas of stealing from someone at this level, she just might be over her head, Nick mused. The question being, who was using who? The other nagging question was, what type business would Majestic Enterprises be in?

"Banking software," the answer came from one of Nick's contacts when he was still doing background checks. "Anyone in that business knows how to move money around. I'd say he probably has some very rich clients. Entertaining would no doubt be an ongoing activity." Ruth Lambert would fit in with that crowd. She always liked to stay close to the money. Nick wondered if she knew how dangerous Mister Benjamin Sigler might be? For that matter did he know how dangerous his entertainment chairman was?

Nick found a motel just over the canal bridge from Pier 66. "Not sure how long I'll be staying. Maybe a week," Nick told the desk clerk. He decided to examine Majestic Enterprises and its activities a little more closely. After all, that was his past activity before retiring. He still had his contacts.

Majestic Enterprises occupied a small office on the sixth floor in the financial district of Fort Lauderdale. Nick expected to see something more impressive. The young receptionist was impressive. She looked like a model, dressed in expensive attire, diamond studs and a beautiful face that could be on any of a dozen magazines. Cleavage was moderate with her white silk blouse. Back to the smile, perfect teeth. Wow! Nick produced one of his former business cards that indicated his investigations agency.

"Mr. Sigler is out of the country at the moment. I don't expect him to return until sometime next week," she said showing a great smile. "Can I tell him what it is you are here for?"

She indicated that the firm just dealt with banking institutions.

"Is this your headquarters?" The reception area was nicely appointed, just smaller than he expected. There was a hallway behind the reception desk that led to other offices well hidden.

"We have several offices, one in the Cayman Islands and one in Mexico City. Mr Sigler travels between all three at different intervals, so he's difficult to catch without an appointment. Perhaps I can help you until I hear from him."

Oh yeah, that would be very nice, Nick thought. He didn't see an engagement ring and wondered what other services she might be providing for old Ben. He wondered if there was any competition with Ruth.

Nick explained that his company did comprehensive background checks on key people in sensitive areas, like those involved with government contracts. This was a stretch since he was now retired. "We can offer those same services for those in banking."

"That does sound like something Mister Sigler might be interested in, particularly with new clients."

"Since I'm new to the Fort Lauderdale scene, I'll bet you could recommend a nice restaurant that serves a good steak and has an excellent bartender."

"There are quite a few nice places that fit that goal."

"Which one would you select?"

"Is this your way of asking me out for dinner and drinks?"

"You are a very perceptive lady." *Yeah, old Nickie was back in town, sung to the tune of, Mack the Knife.*

#

Lauren said, "I'm a Miami girl. Born and raised there, went to college there. I was a cheerleader for three years. Married a football player who was almost a star quarterback until he busted a knee. Then everything changed. He became bitter and took his frustrations out on me. He put me in the hospital and that's where I met Ben." It wasn't mister Sigler now.

"You met him in the hospital?" They were on their second drink at a quiet place known as Taste of Paris. Nick was truly enjoying her company. "Was he having surgery?"

"Yes, he was recuperating from a ruptured stomach ulcer. We met in the patient lounge. He was genuinely concerned about my future and advised me to get a divorce, not return home. I was afraid to go home, didn't have any other place to go. Both my parents are dead. Ben asked a lot of personal questions. The next day he told me it would be safe to return home. He had a friend pay a visit to Jake, that's my now ex-husband who immediately moved out. I think Ben's friend scared him, and he wasn't easily scared of anybody."

"How long ago was that?"

"Three years ago. My divorce was final in six months after Jake left. Ben helped with that, too. His lawyer handled everything."

"Do you still keep in touch with Jake?"

"No. I haven't heard a word from hm. I don't even know where he lives, and frankly, I don't care. I had a lot of work done on my face." Nick couldn't tell.

"I guess you like working for Ben."

"He's the best. I owe him a lot."

"Have you seen his yacht?"

"Oh yeah, that's his big boy toy. He loves that boat and uses it all the time. It's his second home. And he loves to entertain. That's why his clients think so highly of him."

"What about his wife and family?"

"She lives in Costa Rica with the kids. He visits them a couple times a year."

Lauren didn't mention a boyfriend. Like Pam on the rescue boat, she was way too young to be a serious companion, but for a weekend…maybe.

"Look, I didn't ask you to have dinner with me to discuss Ben, but I'd like to suggest that it would be to his advantage to know exactly who he was dealing with, particularly with new clients. Does the company deal with just banks, or are there some private investors as well?"

"That's a separate company. His main activity is providing special software for banks so that they can safely transfer money and not get hacked. We provide a unique firewall that is totally secure. So, tell me about you, Nick. Where are you from originally?"

She did an excellent shift of subject. Nick told her about some of his more exciting exploits as a detective. She listened intently, focusing on his lips like a lip reader. For a moment Nick wished he was a younger man.

After consuming delicious steaks, done to perfection, they opted for a brandy for dessert.

"Would you like to come back to my place?" Lauren asked.

"I have to stop back at the office first to check messages. I'm on call with Ben twenty-four, seven."

Nick waited in the car for Lauren. Lights were on in the

office so people were still working. So far, Nick had learned that Ben had several different companies, all related to money and investments, particularly foreign investments, which were difficult to tract. And, he had some ready muscle! Nick had to be careful. Ben would no doubt check him out. He'd contact his former company, the one he sold, and ask them to pretend he was still employed there, should Ben or Lauren make an inquiry. Otherwise, he could be in big trouble as an imposter.

Nick had several secret resources he used for high-priority and sensitive subjects where a background check might reveal a security breach. One resource had a tap into FBI files using highly sophisticated routing procedures. Anyone back-checking would think it was the Chinese hacking.

Nick's main resource was code-named, Wizard who left Nick a message: Nick, this guy you're looking at is from Venezuela originally. Different name now. The original Ben Sigler was a farm machinery distributor in South America. He died in a car accident in eighty-nine. This guy's real name is Edmundo Feliciano Albert. He's suspected of money laundering and selling used military weapons to third world organizations. He's on their watch list, so be careful. They probably have his communications system tapped. If your name gets mentioned, you'll probably get a visit from one of the alphabet organizations.

It was enough for Nick to beg off spending more time with Lauren. He used an unexpected emergency as an excuse. Whenever the FBI was involved, headaches soon followed. Nick didn't need that. Ben, or Edmundo was a dude to avoid at all costs. He might be overly protective of his property. His property being Lauren. And Ruth, well she had better have an escape plan ready. These Latin American dudes played by a different set of rules, their rules!

Nick hadn't mentioned where he was staying. He hadn't used the motel phone, either. He used his laptop and cellphone. Wizard's email message to Nick had encryption for added security. It automatically erased after the message was read.

It came as no surprise when later the next day, while Nick was taking a quick nap, two suits knocked on his door. Nick didn't have to invite them in, they pushed him aside, flashed their credentials, walked in and sat down in the only two chairs in the room. That left Nick standing. He decided to sit on the edge of the bed.

"Okay, Nick tell us what exactly your interest in Ben Sigler is?" one of the suits asked.

Nick figured they had Ben's office under surveillance, probably followed Nick and waited for just the right time for a surprise visit.

"It's a very strange story, one you probably won't believe," Nick said getting comfortable on the bed, crossing his legs.

"You're right, we probably won't, but give it a shot anyway."

"This goes back fifteen years. I was a detective in the Detroit suburbs of…."

"Is this going to have a happy ending?" one of them asked, tapping his foot on the floor impatiently.

It was all about Ruth. She was dangerous and always would be. She was currently mixed up with a guy the FBI was tracking. If she got a whiff of what was really going on, she'd disappear. She had a habit of doing that. It took Nick two hours to tell the whole story. Searching for Ruth, was it a hobby or an obsession? Explaining the series of events sounded more like a fantasy. Nick had to agree. As of the moment, he also agreed, he had no real interest in Ben Sigler or his activities, none!

As for Ruth, he'd file her away as someone who played him. Her memory had haunted him long enough.

End

About The Author, Richard Standring

Writing has been his hobby since the early '80s. He writes essays, mysteries, poetry, short stories and more recently, flash fiction. He also writes magazine articles. His career in advertising started with several ad agencies in Pittsburgh, PA and later, transitioned to industrial magazine publishing. His other hobby, flying. 25 years dancing among the clouds, searching and finding adventure. Summerville, SC is where he hides from the drama of bigger cities he's known.

I've done my derring-do,
And I've learned a thing, or two,
If you want to hear my story,
I'll tell you a tale, maybe a few.

There was a time when I would fly,
Sometimes low, sometimes, high,
Land below, a patchwork maze,
Oh yes, I still remember those days.

Some stories might scare you,
Other may not be quite true,
I'll save some for another time,
It's what storytellers like to do.

RAS